A TWIST OF OLEANDER

Raven McKray

Keystone

A division of Brownridge Publishing

A Twist of Oleander

ISBN: 978-1-988856-11-7
© 2018 Theresa Wallace-Pregent
as Raven McKray

Cover design by Caitlin Ann Pregent

*Cataloguing in Print information available upon request

Keystone is an imprint of Brownridge Publishing Inc.

Hastings County, Canada, Ontario
August 2019

For Joe

CHAPTER ONE

The buzzing had stopped, but my thoughts were thick like oil, and my legs and arms had turned to lead. I opened my eyes to the too-bright world and took a breath.

"Do you know who you are?" asked a female voice next to me. It took all my energy to turn my head to look at her. In the chair beside the bed sat an Asian woman with kind eyes and shoulder-length black hair. Her voice soothed and strengthened me. She had a clipboard and was writing things on it.

I nodded. "I'm Maddie Malone."

"That's right. I'm Dr. Ng. Do you know where you are now, Ms. Malone?" She stopped writing, her pen poised in the air.

I cringed. "Yes, Carville General Hospital. I… I work here. I'm a nurse."

Dr. Ng nodded. "Great. Can you tell me what happened back in Emergency? You had to triage the patients, is that correct?"

"Yes. I had a lot of things to do, so many people needing help… I snapped. I couldn't think anymore. Nothing made sense."

My mind went back to that terrible moment, back in

triage, when I had drifted down the hallway like a sleepwalker, shrouded in dreams. Around me, other people yelled and made gestures. They moved back and forth, carrying trays full of instruments and bits of paper. I walked past them, keeping my head down. The buzzing inside my brain began: izz-izz-izzz. Fear bit at me like an animal; moving under my skin and burrowing into my stomach.

I remembered all the people in the bright, white room staring at me; their eyes like coals. I was trembling inside. A woman, holding a clipboard, approached me. She spoke, and this time I heard a word I knew—Maddie. I breathed in relief: I had a name. Then the woman thrust a paper into my face. I could read words like, "clopidogrel bisulfate" and "thrombolytic." I knew the shape of the words, their sound, but not their meaning. I tried to eat the words, to make them talk, but the bees in my brain were becoming louder than my thoughts: izz-izz-izzz.

Dr. Ng's soft voice pulled me back to the present: "That's good, Maddie. Go on." I knew what type of doctor she was, even though I had never set foot in this part of the hospital. Dr. Ng. was a psychiatrist. We were in the psych ward.

"I thought I would lose consciousness," I said, my voice a bare whisper. "I was sure I was dying… I was dying inside."

I remembered how the fear-animal thrust its quills into me. The lights above me were too bright; they were daggers to my eyes. I covered my face with my shaking hands. What did these people want from me?

Then, I knew. I was the only one who could help. I had to save these people from Death. I had seen Death that morning. Its claws had been around the face of an old woman; her skin lined and thin as paper. I had tried to help her, but Death was too strong. I had heard Death, too, creeping around the children with bald heads. I had tried to help them, but Death had taken them away.

"IZZ-IZZ-IZZZ-ZIT?" the bees asked me. I shook my head, but it was pointless. The bees wouldn't leave my ears.

Death was coming for me. My breath came harder, faster. My hands and feet tingled. My body vibrated in time with my frenetic heartbeat. I could see Death now, his enormous body draped in shadows. His eyes glowed red from too many tears and from the hell-fires of the damned. He smelled of antiseptic and rotting wounds. His claws were already closing around my heart. I would lose consciousness, and then he would kill me...

"What happened after that?" Dr. Ng prodded.

"I thought I was dying..." I whispered again, trembling, trying in vain to shut out the memory, the moment before the world went black. I remembered how men with white robes came to hold me down, how they stole a quill from Fear and stuck it in my arm.

"They stuck me with needles..." I said in a bare whisper. "Then I woke up here."

Dr. Ng regarded me thoughtfully, then wrote something in her notes. She asked me a few more questions, and I answered them the best I could. Then she gave me medication and left me to sleep.

I drifted in and out of sleep over the next few days. During times of wakefulness, there were no flowers, no cheerful faces saying, "Get well soon." For a while I hoped, and feared, that a few of my coworkers might come to visit: Maybe Rita or Susan, who had commiserated with me about management and day-to-day stresses.

I needn't have worried. No one came. No one wanted to see the woman who had gone crazy. I was alone, and I was in pain. I didn't quite want to die, but I wanted the pain to stop. It was like someone had implanted magnets in my body, and the magnets were pulling me down, down, down to the core of the earth.

Only my mother stood by me. When I was lucid, she was there, sitting beside me. Her eyes were red and puffy, but she still looked beautiful. She even managed a smile.

"It'll be okay, Maddie," she said, patting my hand. I nodded, biting my lower lip. I turned my head away, into the pillow, so she wouldn't have to see me cry.

CHAPTER TWO

"I'm not crazy."

I remember how kindly Dr. Ng. looked when I said this and how serious she was. "No, you're not. Take the medication, get on a regular schedule, and you'll be fine."

I will be fine, I repeated to myself. Over time, I came to believe that; not because Dr. Ng had said it, but because I was stubborn. I had always been goal-driven, and now it was clear what I needed to do. I would learn more about myself, who I was and what I wanted. I would walk out of the hospital a new person, a stronger person, but first, I would have to face the firing squad.

I went down to the nurses' room to collect my things. Most of the nurses, who I had known and worked with for years, hurried away to avoid conversation. Even if they dared speak, they wouldn't meet my eyes. Only my friend, Rita ran to me and gave me a hug.

"Oh, Maddie, I heard you were ill. How are you feeling?" Her eyes searched mine, earnest and empathetic. "I'm feeling better, now. Thanks for asking." This was weird. Why couldn't Rita talk about what had happened? Why couldn't I? There was a solid yet invisible wall between us. We stared at each other, not knowing what to say. Rita sucked in a breath, then put her hand on my shoulder. "I should get back to work. I'm swamped. Come back soon, okay? It's not the same here without you."

I hugged her again, tears coming to my eyes. Rita was a good person. I would miss her. On the way out, I glimpsed Cindy, my manager, talking to one of the other nurses across the hall. She caught my eye, and I saw the fear and distaste flicker over her face before she pasted on her sticky-sweet smile. Then she stuck her chin in the air and strode away, not bothering to say anything. I had never been one of her favorite people, but I didn't expect this treatment. Was I so insignificant I wasn't worth the time of day?

I scraped my self-worth off the floor and made for the exit. My mother was waiting by the door. She stood up and put an arm around me. I leaned on her a little. She smelled like lavender. My beautiful mother, always poised, always calm, always self-contained. She was wearing her full-length trench-coat with a silk paisley scarf and gold lapel-pin. Her hair was in blonde curls—not a hair out of place. How did she always look so perfect? I was a wreck. My long dark hair needed a good combing and a wash. I had barely had enough energy to get dressed, let alone dress well.

Mom helped me to the car. We drove to a coffee shop down the road, and Mom bought me a steaming hot cup. I took the cup, along with the new orange pills Dr. Ng had given me. I sank back in the passenger's seat while Mom drove me home.

"Did Dr. Ng tell you when you can go back to work?" asked my mother, glancing over at me. I shook my head and took a deep breath. "I'm not going back," I said. "At least, not yet. Stress is a huge trigger for me."

My mother nodded, biting her lower lip. She was disappointed. I was, too. I had loved being a nurse, at least in the beginning. I loved helping people, making a difference in their lives. Then something changed. The life-or-death decisions, the handling of medications, the catheterizations, the demands of long hours through the night, the anguished faces of the needy, it all became overwhelming. I wanted to help, yet I felt powerless. I didn't know how to help myself or others. This whole situation was new for me. I had always been so independent. Now, I was the patient, the one needing care. I needed quiet. I needed to heal. But how?

Mom provided the answer. After we had been on the road for a while, she patted my hand and said, "You know, honey, maybe you should visit your Aunt Cassie and your Uncle John out in Kenowa, while you figure things out. I'm sure it would thrill them to have you there, and the fresh air might do you some good. I could phone Cassie, when we get back to your place."

I stared out the car window at the dirty, noisy, city streets. As usual, Mom was right. The summers I had spent at Green Briar— the cattle ranch belonging to Aunt Cassie and Uncle John—had been some of the happiest times of my life. My mind conjured up familiar images; I could see the endless forests, the rock-cuts along the country roads of northern Ontario, the soulful eyes of cattle dotting the fields, the rickety old hayloft, and Alex, the brown-haired, blue-eyed neighbor's boy who had been my childhood friend. This was exactly what I needed, a trip into the forested hills of Kenowa—population: seven hundred.

CHAPTER THREE

The drive to Kenowa was like a journey to another world. The car was swallowed up by deep, shadowed valleys, then spit out again over forested hills and rust-colored slabs of rock. Kenowa was in the Canadian Shield, the name given to an ancient, worn-down mountain chain. The mountains in the distance never reached a significant height; they resembled mountains in miniature, crested with tall trees.

I arrived at Uncle John and Aunt Cassie's ranch feeling like a caged bird just discovering her freedom. A warm autumn sun shone overhead as I rolled down the long driveway flanked by elm trees. Their leaves flashed orange and gold. It was as beautiful as I remembered from my teenage days. A wooden sign said, "Welcome to Green Briar." Another sign nailed to a great oak said, "The Jones Family". Beyond the trees, cattle dotted the vast fields. Rising out of this landscape, an impressive stone house sprawled out on one level. Beyond that I surveyed acres and acres of forest.

I parked the car by an old wooden fence and followed rough-hewn stone pavers to the front door. When I stepped over the threshold, I looked into the mild eyes of my Aunt Cassie. "Maddie!" she said, beaming. "Is that you? You're all grown up.

How old are you now?"

"I'm twenty-six, Aunt Cassie."

My aunt gave me a warm hug, then held me by the shoulders as she stared me up and down. "What a beautiful young lady you are!"

I held back the tears as I smiled. I glanced over her kind face, her steel-grey hair and her thin frame draped in a wool sweater she had knitted herself. My heart wrenched. Aunt Cassie looked older. She was more grey, more lined, and yet somehow more beautiful than I remembered.

"It's good to see you too, Aunt Cassie. Thanks for letting me stay." My words seemed inadequate. How could she know how much I appreciated this? How could she understand the darkness I had experienced?

"Anytime, Maddie,." Aunt Cassie led me into the house. "You know your Uncle John and I could never have children and you've been like a daughter to us. I've always wanted you to feel like this is your home, too: your home-away-from-home. Don't feel obligated to do anything, okay? Just rest and feel better."

I nodded, tears spilling down my cheeks. My mind drifted back to my recent trauma and the frigid reception I had received from many of my coworkers after my stay in the hospital. I knew Aunt Cassie wouldn't treat me that way, but I still wasn't ready to talk about the elephant in the room.

Aunt Cassie seemed to understand. She smoothed my hair and let me cry on her shoulder. Then she ushered me into the big farmhouse kitchen. She sat me down at the kitchen table and served me tea and warm buttered scones.

Aunt Cassie had grown up in England and a good hot tea was her solution to every problem. Funny thing is, she was often right about its healing power: Aunt Cassie's tea made everything seem better. Tight muscles relaxed, conversation flowed and troubles became more manageable with each steaming hot cup.

"I'm sorry Uncle John isn't here to see you," Aunt Cassie said, pouring the black liquid into fine china teacups. "Alex and Randy Bateman came this morning to help John with the cattle drive, and they won't be back for a few hours yet."

"Alex is still working here at Green Briar?" I stirred sugar into my tea. I was a little annoyed to feel a rush of adrenaline at the mention of Alex Bateman. Alex had been my childhood friend, and my first love. That was ancient history, but I often wondered what he was doing and I looked forward to seeing him again.

Aunt Cassie smiled. "Yes, he is such a good help to John. Now that John is getting older, Alex handles all the tough stuff. I don't know what John and I would do without him. He runs the ranch now. His brother Randy helps, too. Do you remember Randy?"

I nodded. I knew Alex's brother, but he hadn't hung out with us much as kids. Randy had autism, and although he was smart and fun to talk to, he preferred his own company most of the time.

As I looked around the kitchen, I couldn't help smiling. Everything was black and white, like the cows in the pasture: from its painted wood floor to the ceramic tile on the walls. It was a testament to how much Aunt Cassie loved her life here at Green Briar. I finished my tea and scones and then rested my head on my arm. My head felt so heavy. My eyelids drooped.

Aunt Cassie looked at me with concern. "You poor thing, you must be exhausted after your long drive! You know where the guest cottage is, why don't you go down there now and have a nap? I cleaned it up for you this morning, so everything's nice and cozy. Just needed a little dusting and some fresh sheets."

"That sounds wonderful." I pushed myself away from the table with an effort. I gathered up my stuff. "Thanks again for everything, Aunt Cassie. I've missed you and Uncle John so much."

"No problem at all, honey. We've missed you, too." Aunt Cassie gave my arm a squeeze. Then, she hesitated, something on her mind.

"Can you make sure to come back up to the house around five o'clock? I've invited a few people over for dinner." Her cheeks reddened. She blurted, "It's just a small get-together, Maddie, nothing too fancy. I thought you should meet some people from Kenowa since you'll be staying awhile."

Inwardly, I groaned. Meeting new people was the last thing I wanted to do right now. Still, I knew Aunt Cassie was doing this out of love. As a child I had been shy and awkward; I rarely spoke to anyone outside the family. Aunt Cassie was always encouraging me to "get out and meet new people," while I preferred to hang out in a quiet corner with a good book. Now as an adult, I was much more outgoing, but it touched me that Aunt Cassie still cared about my social life.

I managed a small smile. "That's thoughtful of you, Aunt Cassie. I'll see you back here at five."

When I followed the dirt path to the guest cottage in the thick of the woods, the fallen leaves were crunching and crackling under my feet. Birds rustled and sang in the branches overhead and the sun shone down through the forest canopy, creating islands of gold and pools of shadow. I felt the stress of a thousand days melt away from me with every step.

I was glad I had come to Green Briar, and to Kenowa. This was where I needed to be. I said a quick prayer of thanksgiving. I didn't know what tomorrow would bring, but right now I was content just to be here.

I glimpsed the Jones' guest cottage through the trees. It was just as I remembered it, a beautiful white building with green shutters: picture-perfect.

As I rounded the corner, and the forest cleared, however, I noticed that there was something different about the little guest cottage. I peered at the green roof through the trees and saw tendrils of smoke curling up to the sky. My heart pounded hard at my chest as I realized that the smoke wasn't coming from the chimney. It was coming from the windows!

I dropped my bags and hurried up to the large front window. I could see the flames of a small fire; something unrecognizable was blazing out of control. The fire had not yet caught the cabin walls, but it was on its way. Smoke filled the rooms.

Springing into action, I flung open the door. My medical training helped me to keep my head. I ran in and grabbed the fire extinguisher off the counter and fought to remove the pin. I aimed the extinguisher at the black source of the flames, spraying it back and forth until the fire was out. Then I ran back outside and sank down on a grassy mound, sucking in deep breaths of fresh air.

I was so thankful that I had arrived when I did. A few moments later and the whole cottage would have been up in flames. What caused the fire, I wondered? I remembered Aunt Cassie saying she had been down to the cottage earlier in the day to clean up, but that was hours ago. The cause of the fire had to be more recent than that: I had just managed to put it out before it got out of control.

When my breathing returned to normal, I re-entered the cottage lugging my overnight bags with me. I threw the bags down next to the couch in the front room. Most of the smoke had cleared, but I threw open the front window to freshen the air and clear out the smell.

I inspected some charred and smouldering remains of

something that looked like plastic or wax. I scratched at it with a fingernail: It was definitely wax. Had somebody been lighting candles? The melted remains scarred the top of both the wood stove and the window-sill, once white and now singed with black. I looked around the cottage for any sign of candles or lanterns but found nothing.

I wondered if anyone else from Green Briar used this cottage from time to time, like maybe Randy or Alex. There was a stack of firewood beside the wood-stove. Someone would have to replenish its supply. Could it have been Uncle John? I remembered he liked to go hunting in the woods from time to time. Did he use the cottage when he was out in the forest?

I would have to wait for the answers to these questions. Exhausted, I lay down on the couch. I took my cell phone from my pocket and set an alarm to wake me in two hours. Then I yawned and fell into a deep sleep.

CHAPTER FOUR

I awoke before my alarm, shivering with cold. The front window was still open. Sitting upright on the couch I looked out of the open window into the forest. Through a screen of trees, I saw a streak of rose and orange across the sky, kissing the dove grey clouds. It wasn't dark yet, but already I saw a sliver of the moon through the thin hands of the trees. I got up, stretched and shut the window. Then I ruffled through my bags to find a suitable change of clothes: Might as well look nice for my Kenowa debut.

I examined the small cottage in more detail. I liked it. The hand-sewn curtains around the window were a sunny yellow, with tiny purple and white flowers. A couch on the opposite wall had decorative cushions made of the same material, as did the tablecloth on the little breakfast table by the front window.

There was a kitchen, dining area, and living room, besides a small bathroom with a shower. There was also a fair-sized bedroom in the back. I went back to the front room and grabbed my overnight bags. Then I returned to the back bedroom and unpacked.

I sat on the four-poster double bed piled high with cushions and stared at myself in the armoire mirror. A stranger stared back at me. I had gained a few pounds since I started my medication. I had the height and build to handle it, but I didn't like it. My long dark hair was all over the place and needed a wash. The almond eyes that blinked back at me were red and puffy. Sighing, I pulled a bottle out of my overnight bag and deposited three orange pills into the palm of my hand. I popped them into my mouth and headed into the bathroom for a glass of water and a shower.

When I had showered and dressed, I headed outside to the ranch house. I felt better in my long navy skirt, white camisole and lacy blue shawl. My hair fell in loose waves around my shoulders. I was ready to face people again, except for the knot of anxiety sitting in the pit of my stomach.

This was the first social event I had attended since I had my manic episode. Aunt Cassie had called it a "small get-together", but I suspected it would be a little more than that. My Aunt Cassie loved to entertain. I assured myself that it would be okay; that I could do this. These people wouldn't have any expectations of me. They didn't know me. This was my fresh start.

I picked my way through the trees, feeling the solemn silence wash over me like a river's tide. I paused, listening. It was a comfort. The Forest was a sentient creature, the silence its voice — calming and comforting. It spoke through the rustling of its branches, the trembling of its leaves, and the cries of its birds.

Emerging from the forest, I stepped past sumac and oak-leaf hydrangea bushes and strode up the grassy slope leading toward Green Briar. At the top of the hill I followed the winding cobblestone path that ran through the house's back garden. As I walked the stone path, I admired the manicured ornamental trees and flowering bushes on either side of me. I knew Aunt Cassie had designed this back-yard garden by herself. What a beautiful retreat she had made! Immersed in these thoughts, I almost ran into a man carrying a large black box.

"Oh, sorry!" I said, jumping out of the way. "That could have been bad!"

"It's all right, Maddie," said the man grinning. He was tall and thin and had a distinguished grey beard and moustache.

"Uncle John!" I cried, hugging his shoulder and almost toppling the box again. "How are you? It's been too long!"

"Don't I know it, dear girl. You sure have grown! Have you been having any more of those ice cream floats?" He winked at me, and I laughed.

Once, when I was a little girl, John and Cassie came to visit and stayed overnight. I had to sleep on the couch, so they could have my room, and it was such a novelty I couldn't sleep. Uncle John couldn't sleep either, and he came downstairs to the kitchen and fixed us both an ice cream float. I laughed and promised not to tell Mom. It was our delicious bit of contraband. Then he tucked me in and told me stories of growing up on the farm until I fell asleep.

"Whenever I have an ice cream float, I have it in honor of you, Uncle John," I teased.

"Well now, I might have root beer and vanilla ice cream in the kitchen if you'd like some."

"Okay," I laughed. "But I think Aunt Cassie would prefer that we have dinner first."

"Well now, I won't tell if you won't!"

I laughed again and opened the back door for him. "What's in the box, anyway?"

"Well, it's top secret, but I can show you if you like," John said, looking smug and mysterious. I smiled.

"Is it one of your amazing wood carvings?"

John grinned and set the box down on the step, removing the lid.

"It's not finished yet, but I might have enough time to get it ready for the Hastings County Woodcarvers' Competition in the spring. It's been a dream of mine to take home the Whimsy Award. Who knows?"

I peered into the box and let out a cry. "Oh, Uncle John! This is beautiful!" It was breathtaking. Much of the wood was still raw, but already there were intricate characters emerging from it: children holding small animals like birds and rabbits and squirrels. The children had pudgy little faces with angelic smiles. I loved it.

"Thank you, Maddie. It's not bad, if I say so myself." He smiled. "I'll put this away then join you for dinner." John carried the box off to the east wing where the spare bedrooms were.

The back door opened to a mud room where I took off my shoes. When I looked up, I caught a brief glimpse of a dark-haired young man walking down the hallway leading to the east wing. The way he walked—with purpose, his head held high—seemed somehow familiar to me. My breath caught in my throat: that couldn't be Alex, could it? All grown up?

With a light heart, I headed to the west wing where the great room was. The smells of turkey pot pie and fresh-baked bread made my mouth water. I bumped into Aunt Cassie. She looked flustered.

"Oh, there you are Maddie!" she said. "Go sit down at the table; everything's ready for you."

"Oh, okay," I said in surprise. "I didn't realize I was late."

Aunt Cassie disappeared into the kitchen and I hurried into the dining area off the kitchen. Seeing the long dinner table I drew in my breath. The table was a work of art. Cassie had outdone herself. Candelabras were burning, and antique red and white English china complemented the rich, wine-coloured tablecloth. Beds of real roses surrounded bottles of Merlot—my favorite red wine—in pinks, yellows, and reds.

I couldn't believe the lengths Aunt Cassie had gone to for me. I was overcome with love and gratitude as I sat down at a place-setting that had my name written in black ink on a white placard.

A few moments later Aunt Cassie came out of the kitchen holding a basket of dinner rolls which she placed on the table in front of me.

"Aunt Cassie, you didn't have to do all this", I said as I stood up and hugged her. My face crumpled into a mess of tears. I couldn't help it. They just spilled out. I felt so stupid and embarrassed and tried to hide my face in my hair. Cassie brushed my hair back out of the way, meeting my eyes. Hers brimmed with kindness and love.

"It's nothing at all, Maddie. You know I enjoy doing this for you. I'm just glad you're here." Her voice, like mine, was a little choked up. "Come sit down now, dear. We have guests coming to meet you."

I shook my head, biting my lower lip. I couldn't understand why. Come and meet the screw-up from the city, I thought. Then I repented: I wouldn't slip into negative thinking again. If nothing else, I was a human being like others. That alone deserved respect. I also had people who loved me.

"The guests should arrive any minute now. Why don't I pour you a glass of wine while you're waiting?"

I nodded, wiping my face with a napkin. Then, my mind went back to the cottage fire.

"Aunt Cassie, did you light any candles at all when you were down at the cottage?"

She frowned. "No, why?"

"No reason. I just wondered, that's all. It smells nice in there, like incense. I guess that's just the wood." I felt bad about my little white lie, but I didn't want to worry her.

While I sat there, sipping my wine and listening to a composition by Philip Glass playing in the background, I began to enjoy myself. I knew this piece well, it was "Duet," from the soundtrack of the movie Stoker. I loved the haunting feel of this music and its sweeping dynamics. The piece started soft and slow, then escalated in volume and tempo. Then this imaginative ride spun out of control: the notes rose faster-and-faster up, reached a thunderous climax, then descended in a free-fall. I hummed along with the tune, unaware of how well that musical journey mirrored my own.

CHAPTER FIVE

I noticed a vague stinging sensation on my wrist and realized that I had burned myself in the fire. Who started it? And why? I would ask Uncle John about it when I got the chance. I would also ask about getting a key for the cottage door. It would make me feel a little better if I could lock up when I left.

The sound of laughter in the hallway interrupted my thoughts. Soon a dazzling presence lit up the room — a small entourage led by Aunt Cassie. The laughter came from a petite girl with a side ponytail wearing a long shirt covered in splashes of bright colour. She had a small space between her two front teeth and her eyes scrunched into slits as she laughed.

A giant of a man in a plaid shirt with long black hair followed the girl with the ponytail. A pair of twinkling black eyes, dome-shaped, peered at me, but the rest of his face sank into heavy jowls, so that apart from his eyes, he looked almost surly.

Close at the giant's side was a tall man in his mid-thirties dressed in a white shirt and black tie. The tie was askew, and the starched shirt unbuttoned at the top. As I looked at him, he looked away, as people always do when they realize they've been staring. Was he studying me? Feeling self-conscious, I pulled my shawl tighter around my bare shoulders.

My aunt flagged me down. "Maddie, this is Alvira Minton," she said, indicating the ponytail girl. "She works at Wren's Bakery and Grill in town."

"Hi," I said, nodding and smiling. Alvira surprised me by grabbing my hand and giving it an enthusiastic shake.

"So glad to meet you!" she said, still shaking my hand. "Cassie talks about you often. She says you're a nurse. I like botany, myself. And microbiology. Working at Wren's helps pay for my studies."

"Are you studying biology?"

"Sure am," she gave a flip of her ponytail. "I'm in fourth year."

"That's great! What will you do after you graduate?"

"Lab work. I can't imagine anything more exciting, can you? There are microscopic beings crawling all over everything. Even a sample of pure water isn't pure at all, is it? It's a universe of unseen creatures."

"You can sit here, Alvira," said Aunt Cassie, interrupting. She pulled out a chair at the end of the table, away from me. I smiled. I guessed Aunt Cassie was trying to save me from an in-depth discussion of germs and microorganisms. I didn't mind the topic, though. And Alvira seemed nice, if a little nerdy.

"I'll put you here, George", Cassie directed the big man in plaid to a spot across the table from me. I peered at George through the flaming candelabras.

"Maddie, this is George Riddleman. He owns the Buck and Bullet in town."

"Hi, how are you?" I said pasting a smile on my face. Hunting was not one of my favorite topics. I sympathized with Bambi, rather than the hunters.

George nodded at me, then sat down. He never looked straight at me, but his eyes flickered a little in my direction, and he twisted his handkerchief in his hands.

"Pleased to meet you, Miss. If there's anything I can do for you, let me know, eh?" He addressed this to the floor. George Riddleman was avoiding my gaze. Since he could look at the men seated around the table, I presumed he had trouble talking to women.

"Thank you, Mr. Riddleman. I will. I know little about hunting and fishing, but maybe you can enlighten me sometime."

George smiled into his plate. "Sure, I can. Just look me up anytime. I'll be at the Buck and Bullet. On Main Street. Can't miss it."

It was awkward talking to someone who never returned my gaze. I stole a glance at the well-dressed man seated beside me. He responded with a smile.

"Clayton Manning," he said, extending his hand.

I took it, feeling a firm, decisive grip. My eyes met intelligent, probing eyes of the brightest blue. Stammering, I told him my name.

"I'm Maddie."

Clayton smiled. "Pleased to meet you, Maddie. I'm the new doctor here in Kenowa."

"Oh, I'm a…"

"Nurse," he finished. "Cassie told me. We're looking for a Nurse Practitioner at the clinic. If you're interested." Clayton's steady gaze was unnerving.

"Oh. Thank you, no. At least, I don't think so." This was getting awkward. I didn't want to bring up the whole issue of my mood disorder, and I wasn't ready for nursing again. Not now… maybe never. So, what could I say that wouldn't sound stupid or evasive? How could I think straight with those bright blue eyes probing me?

I took a great gulp of wine and stared at the table, the silence growing larger like the great gaping mouth of some monster ready to swallow me whole. Aunt Cassie, who chose that moment to bring in a tray of roast chicken, saved me from further discomfort. Uncle John was close behind her bearing a tray of mashed potatoes and gravy and assorted steaming-hot vegetables.

"Alex and Randy are just washing up, but we'll get started," said Cassie setting down the tray as we all made grateful noises. "We have a few more guests coming, but they can't make it for dinner. They'll join us for drinks afterward."

"This looks wonderful, Cassie, thank you!" said Clayton, starting to dish up. We all echoed our thanks. Clayton took up the chicken and offered me first choice.

"Thank you," I said. I wondered if Cassie had told everyone to be so nice. I chased this thought away and took another sip of the merlot, hoping it would help me relax.

Alex and Randy joined us half-way through the dinner. Randy wore a hoodie and kept his head covered and his eyes down. Alex sat beside his brother. It was strange to see Alex as an adult, and I studied him with interest. He had grown tall and his shoulders were broad, muscled from hard work. I saw the same almond-shaped eyes half-covered by a shock of brown hair. He was a young man now but I could still glimpse the boy I once knew in his midnight-blue eyes.

I got my chance to say hi to Alex after dinner, when we all convened in the Great Room for drinks and dessert.

"Do you remember me, Alex?" I said, peering at him through the rim of my wine glass.

"Course I do, Maddie," he said smiling. "Though you've grown up a lot since I last saw you." Alex's gaze flickered over me, and I dropped my eyes, twisting the stem of my wine glass between my fingertips.

"So have you," I said, swirling the red liquid around my glass.

"It's been a long time since we played king-of-the-hayloft out in the barn."

"Too long," said Alex, nodding. "We had a lot of fun times together back then." Still trying to reconcile the boy I knew with the man before me, I studied the cut of his cheekbones, the determined set of his jaw and the fine line of his lips, drawn into an engaging smile.

"Aunt Cassie says you still work here at the ranch. She says John couldn't run things without you."

Alex shrugged. "I do my best. John's the father I never had. I'm sure I told you my old man left Randy and I when we were little. John kind of filled his place. I owe him everything." Alex glanced over at him with affection.

"So whatcha doing these days besides hanging round the barn?" I teased.

Alex flushed. "Well, I'm taking a Master's in geology. I'm writing my thesis when I'm not nursing sick heifers or cleaning out the stalls. It's been tough to focus on writing, though. There have been a lot of sick cows this summer."

"Oh, how come?"

He shrugged his shoulders. "The vet says it could be a virus, but if it is, it's an aggressive one."

I stretched across the table to help myself to a slice of lemon cake and Alex caught my arm.

"What happened here?" he asked, frowning. I looked at the flaming red blister on my wrist.

"Oh, I meant to ask you or John about that," I told him about the fire in the cottage and how I had just put it out in time.

"Do you or Randy use the cottage at all? Could you have left the stove on? I'm not trying to blame you; it's just that I'd feel better knowing."

Alex shook his head, looking concerned.

"Randy and I never use the cottage any more. We stay here at the ranch house when we need to. Otherwise, we stay with our mother. I'm sure you remember my mom. She owns the Kenowa Bed and Breakfast now. That's her over there with the red scarf." I looked around the room and saw a large olive-skinned woman with frizzy hair dressed in a yellow satin blouse and skirt; a red scarf draped around her neck. She was busy talking to Aunt Cassie.

"Well, I wish I knew how it happened. It's a little unnerving," I said, taking a sip of my wine.

The candlelight cast a surreal glow on the table and in the faces of the guests. I caught Alex staring at me like I was something new and wonderful and I smiled. He smiled back.

I looked around the room enjoying a new affection for everyone and everything in it. I forgot about the cottage fire and my fears about my mania returning. At least for this moment, everything was right with the world.

CHAPTER SIX

Aunt Cassie changed the music to Indie folk-rock, and I felt the beat moving through me like some predatory animal I was powerless to overcome. I removed my shawl with a flair. It felt constricting and hot.

The music, the wine and the people were ramping up my mood. In a moment of clarity I sensed the manic beast lurking in the shadows of my mind: I knew I had to be careful. I had taken my orange pills before I left the cottage, but the party atmosphere was causing my thoughts to race and I felt the need to escape.

"Maddie, where are you going?" Aunt Cassie asked, as I headed toward the back door.

"I'm just going out to clear my head, Aunt Cassie. Be back in a few minutes, okay?"

"That's my girl. I was just going to put the kettle on. You're welcome to a nice cup of herbal tea when you come back in." I nodded, feeling my face flush.

I slipped out the sliding glass door of the great room. The outside lights were on, lighting up the garden and the cobblestone walkway. It was cold, but I had been too hot inside, so the effect was refreshing. Sobering.

I sat down on a stone bench and looked at the people talking and laughing inside the house. They looked unreal. It was as if I was watching a movie. I turned my gaze upwards and looked at the night sky; my mind expanded outward. Looking at the stars always made me feel small, but not insignificant. I felt a part of some grand plan, like a voyageur on my way to a great destiny: I just wished I knew what that was.

A noise in the bushes interrupted my thoughts. Who was it? My heart sped up. It couldn't be an animal; I decided. It sounded metallic like something scraping across the stones.

"Who's there?" I asked the darkness. There was no answer, but the noises stopped. The silence was scarier than the noise had been. I had to concentrate on slowing my breathing. Maybe I was a little manic. My overactive imagination was getting the better of me. Just get a grip, Maddie, I told myself.

I rose to my feet and faced the bushes, my heart still pounding. I hesitated, my ears straining to hear any small sound. I heard nothing more.

I hurried toward the house, trying to escape whatever might lurk in the darkness. Just as I reached the door, I almost ran into a dark figure silhouetted against the light. A scream erupted from my throat.

"Whoa, there! It's okay, Maddie. It's just me. I didn't mean to startle you." Clayton Manning put his arms around my shoulders to steady me. His calm strength was like a shelter in a storm.

"Sorry, I'm a little spooked. I thought I heard someone in those bushes."

"Let's have a look. I have a flashlight on my phone."

With Clayton at my side, I felt braver and followed him to the bushes where he swept the light back and forth. He pushed the branches aside, but still, we saw and heard nothing.

"Well, whatever it was, it's gone now. Probably just a raccoon."

"Yeah, you could be right. I guess I'm not used to the wildlife around here," I smiled, feeling foolish.

"You're shivering—here, let me help." Clayton took off his jacket and draped it around my shoulders.

As we sat down together on the stone bench, I could feel his closeness, the warmth of him and his breathing. I stole a glance at him and found him looking at me, too.

"So, what are you doing here, Maddie? You should be inside enjoying the party." Clayton's voice was warm and gentle, like his eyes.

"I'm introverted. A room full of people is overwhelming," I said with a shrug. "Why are you out here?"

"I must confess, I came to find you." Clayton sat back against the bench, putting his hands behind his head. "Cassie tells me you worked at Carville General. I wondered how you enjoyed working in a big city hospital?"

I cringed. "I don't. It's too stressful. I can't stand the hours and the difficult decisions. And I never seem to have enough time for the patients, you know?"

Clayton nodded. "So, you're here at Green Briar for a rest, is that it?"

I sighed, a little louder than I meant to. "Yes. And I need to figure out what to do with the rest of my life. I'm not sure I want to go back… but I don't know what else to do going forward."

Clayton regarded me for a moment. "I think I understand," he said. "Before moving to Kenowa, I lived life in the fast lane. Here, life moves at a slower pace. I have the time to get to know my patients. There's more money and opportunity in the city, but it couldn't make up for what I have here."

"And what's that?" I asked, looking sideways at him.

"Peace of mind." Clayton smiled and the creases around his eyes smiled too. "Come work for me, Maddie. I could use the help. You'd like it, I think. It's a lot different from working in a big city hospital."

I shook my head. "I wish I could say 'yes.' It's a tempting offer, Clayton, but I'll need some time to think about it."

"I understand. I hope you'll consider it, though." Clayton stood up and gave me his hand.

"Come on," he said. "Let's get you back in where it's warm."

"Okay," I said, rising. When he let go of my hand, I still felt the ghost of his touch.

We stepped back in through the sliding glass door, and Clayton guided me over to the wood stove in the great room. He went to get me a drink, and I stared at the fire, listening to the music. It had changed to a soft instrumental guitar piece by Andrew York. I watched the flames dance feeling much calmer than before. Despite my little scare outside on the patio, the fresh air had helped to calm me down. Sometimes I just needed the space to breathe, to stop me from getting too overwhelmed. Also, I noticed that being with Clayton had had a calming effect on me. Maybe it was his confidence; the way he faced everything with a calm certainty. And he was, I had to admit, more than a little attractive.

CHAPTER SEVEN

A slight movement beside me alerted me to the fact I wasn't alone. A woman in a wingback armchair sat beside me covered with blankets and sipping her tea. She looked to be in her late fifties or early sixties, with greyish-brown hair. She swept her hair up at the back to keep it out of her face, but fine wisps of it spilled out framing her large violet eyes. I noticed she was one of those lucky women with long thick lashes, which meant she never had to put on make-up.

"Hi," she said, meeting my eyes. "I'm Tuppence Millard, a friend of Cassie. You're Maddie Malone, right?"

I nodded. "And you're the artist who painted that," I pointed to the winter scene on the wall above Cassie's favorite armchair.

"The same," she smiled.

"It's beautiful. And I'm not just saying that. I noticed it earlier today and admired the style. It's so original. Surreal. I don't know how you do it. The trees look almost human, the way they caress the sky."

Tuppence stared at me. "You're right, that was what I was going for. I wanted to show nature as a living entity, not something to use or exploit." She hesitated. Then she asked: "Do you paint, Maddie? You seem like an artist type."

"Do I?" I asked, surprised. "No, I don't paint. I write poetry, though. Perhaps that gives me more insight than the average observer."

Tuppence nodded, looking thoughtful. "Yes, I think you're right. Poets and artists share a unique vision of things; our feelings run deep. You know, I have a gallery in town. You should come over sometime, and we'll talk."

"I'd like that," I said smiling. I meant it. Tuppence was easier to talk to than most people.

Clayton approached holding a cup of chamomile on a saucer. He pulled up a chair beside me.

"Clayton, do you know Tuppence?" I asked, as he handed me the cup.

"I do," he said smiling over at her. "I have several of her paintings in my office. She has a spectacular talent for landscapes."

"Flattery will get you everywhere," said Tuppence laughing and rising from her chair. She was wearing a multi-colored poncho and its fringes dangled and danced in front of the fire.

"Come sit here, Dr. Manning. I'll leave you two lovebirds alone, shall I? I'm going for a stroll."

"But we're not…" I sputtered. It was getting too warm by the fire.

Clayton just smiled, his blue eyes sparkling. I liked the crow's feet crinkling the corners of his eyes. "Why not?" his dancing eyes seemed to say.

I changed the subject. "Sorry about freaking out outside. I've been on edge since I came here. There was a fire in the guest cottage when I got to it, and I'm not sure how it started."

Clayton frowned. "That sounds serious. Was anybody in there this morning who could have started it by accident?"

"I'm not sure. I thought maybe Alex or Randy had been in there, but Alex says he never goes that way. Cassie was in there cleaning up this morning, but she said she never touched the stove. I haven't asked Uncle John yet."

"Well, come on. Let's ask him." He rose from his chair and held out his hand to help me out of mine.

We made our way around the crowded room, stopping to talk to a few people on the way. It seemed like everyone present knew and liked Dr. Manning and had something they wanted to tell him. I let Clayton do all the talking. I preferred to hang back in the shadows, my eyes scanning the room for my uncle.

While Clayton was busy talking to George Riddleman, I spotted a man's figure in a dark corner, head down, body slumped over a small decorative table. It was close by the sliding glass door that lead to the back terrace. I could tell right away something was very wrong: The man was moaning and clutching his stomach.

My own stomach wrenched. Fear clutched at my heart: I knew that voice well.

"Uncle John?" I cried, rushing to his side. "Are you okay?"

Clayton heard me cry out and wasted no time. He sprinted across the room.

"John, can you hear me?" Clayton asked, taking John's pulse. His eyes were shut tight in pain but he moaned in response.

"His pulse is erratic," Clayton said, his face grim.

"What's wrong?" I asked, frightened and in shock.

"Look at his skin, Maddie," said Clayton, pointing. It was then I saw the bright red rash. It looked like some kind of allergic reaction.

I pulled out my cell phone and called 911. "My uncle is having a severe reaction to something. Send an ambulance!" I told the operator about the arrythmia, the abdominal pain and the rash. I also explained there was a doctor present and gave them the address of Green Briar.

Things were a blur after that. Cassie ran to John's side. "John!… John, what's wrong?" She turned to us, panic in her eyes. "Can't you do something?" she shrieked. But there was nothing we could do until the paramedics arrived.

I tried to calm her down and give John and Clayton some space. Everyone feared for John's safety; I had no trouble clearing the room. By the time the ambulance arrived, it was evident that this was no mere allergic reaction: my Uncle John started having convulsions on the floor.

Everything felt unreal. Clayton and Cassie went with Uncle John in the ambulance to the nearest hospital, which was thirty kilometers away. They called an hour later, saying we had lost him. Just like that. I had only been to Green Briar for one day, and the face of Death again haunted my world.

CHAPTER EIGHT

Everyone processes grief in different ways. I put mine on a shelf and take it out later, to deal with as a delicate explosive—with the utmost care. Most often, in the moment of shock, I remember my training. I deal with the situation. It's afterward I fall apart. On this occasion, I stayed calm and sane. For Aunt Cassie's sake.

The next day we sat huddled in the great room by the wood stove: Cassie, Alex, Randy, and I. All of us were grieving and trying to make sense of it all.

"I don't understand it," moaned Cassie, shaking her head. "He had no allergies. None I knew of. What would do that to him?"

"Allergies can develop any time, even severe ones," I said. "Plus, we won't know what happened until the autopsy. The symptoms are also consistent with poisoning."

"Food poisoning?" cried Cassie. "I can't believe that! I prepared the food fresh, myself. And besides, everyone ate the same thing."

"He didn't eat or drink anything different from the rest of us?"

Aunt Cassie thought for a moment. "Only herbal tea. John loves lemon ginger. It was his favorite." Cassie dissolved into tears again, and I put my arms around her.

"Maybe you should get some sleep, Aunt Cassie."

Cassie shook her head. "I can't sleep. I don't want to be alone. Oh God, I don't want to be alone!" She put her head in her hands and sobbed. Alex threw me a pleading look that said: "Do something, Maddie." I understood what he meant. I put on my nurse's manner.

"Okay, Cassie. You can sleep near the fire here," I said. "You don't have to worry; we're not going to leave your side. I'll put the kettle on, and Alex will get you some blankets."

I hurried into the kitchen, looking for something to help her sleep. Maybe she had some chamomile tea hanging around? I went over to Cassie's tea cupboard. That's when something caught my eye, something wedged into a corner, missed by a washcloth. Somehow, in Cassie's immaculate kitchen it was odd to see a tiny flower petal like that, sitting close by the sugar bowl.

"Now that's strange," I said to myself. There were no flowers in the kitchen, and the only flowers at the dinner table had been roses. This was a small, pale-pink petal. It was still fresh. My mind leaped. Could this be important somehow? Was this the mysterious allergen? I looked around for something to keep it in and found some cellophane wrap. Using a paper towel, I picked the flower off the counter and wrapped it in cellophane.

It had to be a bad dream, I kept thinking. I clung to the normal routines so I wouldn't have to think about the horror of the moment. I washed my hands in automatic mode, found the chamomile and filled the kettle.

While waiting for the kettle to boil, I thought about the flower petal. Its shape and size and color had looked familiar. Was this one of those plants in the back garden by the terrace, one of the flowering shrubs I had admired earlier? I was almost positive I had seen the same flowers there before. This would require some investigating.

I finished making the tea and brought it out to Aunt Cassie.

Alex had her wrapped in blankets. She was nodding off, even before I set her cup of chamomile down on the table beside her armchair.

While Cassie slept, I turned to Randy and Alex, who were both looking pale and scared. I felt a pang of pity for them, realizing that they, too, had lost a father figure, and a good friend.

"Do you guys want some tea, too?" I offered. "Or maybe something stronger?" They shook their heads.

"No thanks, Maddie," said Alex, looking into the distance. "I'll miss him, you know?" I nodded.

"I don't know what we'll do without him," said Randy, his eyes down, his fingers twisting his sleeve.

"I know. He was such a big part of your lives," I said, looking from one to the other. "We'll all miss Uncle John. Even though I didn't see him that often, we were close. He played a big part in my life after Dad died." The guys nodded. Everyone understood.

I sat down on an armchair across from them. "I can only imagine what Aunt Cassie is feeling right now. Uncle John was her entire world."

Alex straightened. "I know. I'll look after her. I'll do the best I can, but it'll be tough to manage without John."

I flashed a smile at him, feeling a lump rise in my throat. Alex would look after Aunt Cassie. You could depend on him to do the right thing, to be there when you needed him. He had always been that way.

I thought again about the way Uncle John died and remembered the pink petal in my pocket. "Do either of you guys know what that flowering shrub is in the backyard, the one with the pink petals?" I asked.

Alex frowned. "I think I know the one you mean. It's called oleander, and it's poison for the cattle. Although, I think John told me they once used it in Native medicine. Not to eat, though.

Just for the skin—ulcers and such."

I grabbed my cell phone out of my skirt pocket and did a quick search for oleander. What I found made my blood run cold.

"This plant is deadly," I said in a hushed voice. "And I found some of it in the kitchen." The Bateman brothers stared at me with white faces. I typed in the phone number for the police department in Reidsville. My hands shook as I held the phone and when I spoke, my voice shook a little too.

"I need to speak to an officer right away. This is an emergency."

CHAPTER NINE

I did not sleep for days. I paced and paced, like a caged tiger. My mind kept going over the night of the party. What had happened to my dear sweet Uncle John? Was it true someone had poisoned him with oleander flowers?

The police came and searched the place from top to bottom. They took the petal I had found into evidence. They also took John's cup away for further analysis. The police asked several questions. They wanted to know if John had seemed depressed or if he had quarrelled with anyone. Then they left, and I heard nothing more after that.

I was hoping for some word. One way or another to break the intense waiting. I was watching the clouds gather, waiting for the inevitable storm. And where was the good doctor, Clayton Manning? You'd think he'd come check on Cassie, give her something to help her mental state. Okay, I admit it; I wanted to see Clayton for more selfish reasons.

Aunt Cassie walked around in a daze. She seemed to have broken with reality, oblivious to the heinous fact that either someone had wanted John dead, or he had wanted to take his own life. Both were too horrible to contemplate.

Somehow, I didn't believe that John would take his own life, though. He always had such an appreciation for life. Even if he had wanted to commit suicide, why would he choose a poison that would put him in such terrible pain?

I took my pacing to the garden where I continued to walk in circles, my mind spinning in time to the rhythm of my feet. I turned to the oleander bushes, once so beautiful to my mind, with hateful passion.

"How could you do this to my Uncle?" I accused them, willing them to wither and die. I knew this was ridiculous. It wasn't the fault of the plant. Someone had murdered him and I would move heaven and earth to find out who it was.

"Excuse me, Miss," said a woman's voice behind me. I whirled around.

"Inspector Trent," she said, flashing her badge. "Are you Maddie Malone?" I nodded.

"I need to ask you some questions. I understand you found the bit of oleander in the kitchen?"

"Yes. On the kitchen counter, in the corner by the tea cupboard."

Inspector Trent stared at me. I flushed. "I wanted to make a chamomile tea for my Aunt Cassie. She was in a terrible state, and I thought the tea might relax her."

"What was your relationship to the deceased?" Detective Trent pulled out a notebook and pen.

"He was my uncle. We were close: He was a father figure to me after my dad died."

I studied Detective Trent as she wrote this down. She did not look like my idea of a police officer. Meeting her on the street in different circumstances I would have thought she was a real estate agent or business woman. Or a model, if she was wearing the right clothes. She had shoulder-length blonde hair, blue eyes, a straight nose and was wearing a smart brown suit that emphasized her curves. Detective Trent was all business in her manner, however. An overachiever, I thought. I wasn't wrong. But I wasn't prepared for what came next.

"Did Cassie and John get along?" she asked, arching one eyebrow at me. "Did Cassie have any reason to fear him, for instance?"

I stared at her in shock. "No!" I said, getting angry. "My Uncle John was the kindest, sweetest man ever! He was a gentle giant, and always my Aunt Cassie had the last say."

"They were having financial problems. Did they ever argue in front of you?"

"I don't like what you're insinuating Inspector. I've never seen them argue or have any negative words to say to each other ever!" I said, my voice rising in pitch. Then I spotted a familiar face coming through the sliding glass door.

"Clayton!" I cried, sounding a little too relieved. He looked amused.

"Is the big bad inspector bothering you?" he asked mock-sternly. Then he turned to the blonde detective. "How are you, Rebecca?" he asked with a smile.

"I'm fine, Clayton." Rebecca grinned. "Just trying to get a handle on this case." So, the poker-faced inspector could smile, I thought to myself. I felt a twinge of jealousy. Just how well did Clayton know the beautiful detective? Well enough to call her by her first name.

I pushed that thought away as soon as it came.

"Clayton, she thinks Cassie might have had something to do with John's death!"

"She's just doing her job, Maddie. I'm sure she's not accusing Cassie of anything."

"I need Mrs. Jones to come down to the station and make a statement. It's just a formality at this point. Several eyewitnesses have said that she was the one who prepared Mr. Jones' tea, and as his wife, it is normal for her to be a person of interest."

"I don't believe this!" I said, starting to lose my cool.

"It's okay, Maddie. Let's let the detective do her job. Walk with me?" He asked, taking my hand. I hesitated. Then, I nodded. How comfortable Clayton's hand felt in mine. How calming he was. He must be an excellent doctor, I thought. I allowed him to lead me away toward the forest.

The wind sang as it caressed the branches of the trees. I closed my eyes, letting Clayton lead me down the path to the guest cottage. As my therapist had taught me to do, I focused on my breathing. We walked in silence for a long stretch, and I soon felt more like myself again.

I marveled that I could feel so comfortable with another person that speech was unnecessary. It was enough to be together, to let the gold and red leaves and the sunlight soak up our thoughts, our emotions. With some surprise, I realized we were still holding hands, and had been this whole time. It felt natural, like it had always been this way. I looked up into Clayton's face, and he smiled. I smiled back, but took my hand away. Proceed with caution, I decided.

"Feeling any better?" he asked, leaning in just a little.

I nodded. "Guess it's only natural for the police to suspect Cassie, but I know she's innocent."

"I know. It's only a matter of time before the police come to that conclusion, but they must rule out every possibility, you know? Anyway, I have it on good authority that they think it was suicide."

"Suicide!" I stopped and stared at him. "That's not possible! My Uncle John would never kill himself!"

"It's more possible than your aunt having killed him, isn't it? John was a quiet man, who kept his feelings to himself. And he knew about the dangers of oleander. He had Cassie plant the bushes well away from the cattle."

"Yes, but he loved life so much! And Aunt Cassie! He would never do that to her!"

Clayton looked at me, his eyes kind. "Maddie, you can't always see the depths of sadness a person endures. It's not outside the realm of possibility."

I fell silent. He was right. Depression was a horrible thing: I too had felt the hopelessness, the despair like a crushing weight on my soul. I remembered the physical and emotional pain, and how I had wanted to stop it. But instead of harming myself, I sought help. As a nurse, I knew some medicines could help. And there were people I could turn to. I was glad that somehow I was able to hold life sacred, even a life of pain. I thought Uncle John was like that too.

I took a deep breath in. "Okay, I concede that it's possible. I haven't been around enough to know for sure what John was thinking or feeling. But I know that depressed people don't get up at the crack of dawn to work on their ranch. They don't cut firewood and crack jokes and make everyone around them laugh. Uncle John did all those things up to the day he died. He loved life. He was even working on a woodcarving to enter in the spring competition—it was his dream! No, I think there has to be another explanation."

We had reached the door of the guest house. A large part of me wanted to invite Clayton in, but I was too afraid. How could I trust my feelings around him, when I had so many things in my mind and heart to sort out? Also, I was so tired I couldn't think straight. I think Clayton might have been feeling the same way because for the first time he looked a little uncertain.

"I've got to get back to town," he said. "But I'll call you later. Try to get some sleep, Maddie, okay? Take care of yourself."

I nodded and opened the door without looking back.

CHAPTER TEN

For two days I slept around the clock, unable to resist a steady torrent of dreams. In the short bursts of wakefulness the sun burned my eyes, and the moon sealed them shut. My muscles were jelly.

I was never hungry. In the short moments between sleep I crawled to the bathroom. I even laid in the bath and stared at the ceiling and thought about the night Uncle John died. I played it over and over in my mind, like a film noir. Then my consciousness dissolved back into the dream and the film played on, but with distorted sounds and images. I saw the key players in a large dark room: The pony-tailed Alvira, playing with bacterial cultures. George, the hunter, swinging a large rifle around while studying the floor; Alex and Randy, bringing in firewood and wielding an axe; Aunt Cassie and Thalia laughing over cups of tea, faces contorted and eyes wide. I saw the artist Tuppence Millard painting her face, her fake red mouth twisted into a smile. The handsome Dr. Manning was there too, except he had vampire teeth and mesmerizing blue eyes. In the middle of the floor was a dead fish, and I danced around it crying: "Who has killed it! One of you is lying!" The macabre dream went on for an eternity.

"Maddie?" The knock on the cottage door grew louder, more insistent. My eyelids flickered. Try as I might, I couldn't move. The effort was too great. My body was a dead weight in the tub.

"Maddie, it's Clayton Manning. Could you please let me in? I just want to talk."

My mind held on to the name. Clayton. Clayton Manning. Through thick clouds of dreaming, I conjured an image: beautiful blue eyes, kind, calm, strong... doctor.

The last word brought other images and fear into the dream. The dream took on a nightmarish quality. There was a hospital, white and stark.

"Relax, Miss Malone. I've brought you something to help you sleep," the voice from my memory said. I wanted to scream: It wasn't fair; there was nothing wrong with me. It was everyone else who had the problem. I wasn't. Crazy. Yes, yes, I was. I needed my pills. I wanted to die. There I was, lying dead on the operating table. But it wasn't me lying dead on the hospital table; it was someone else. It was John. Uncle John was dead. But somehow his mouth was moving, and he was trying to tell me something, trying to warn me.

"Maddie, please! Let me in! I want to talk to you!" Clayton pleaded. The knocking echoed in my brain. My mind awoke to the present moment. I coaxed my body over the edge of the bath. My feet slid down to the bare floor. Almost there. I dried and smoothed my tangled hair and stumbled over to the hook on the wall where I kept my bathrobe. The knocking continued, relentless, beating like a drum in my brain. The floor swayed like a swing bridge over a great chasm. Through the bedroom, across the living room floor. Almost there. I unlatched the door and opened it a crack. The blue eyes were there, looking through me, full of concern.

"Maddie!" he said opening the door. I almost collapsed into his arms. With a firm yet gentle hand, he led me to the couch and held both my hands in his. His warmth seeped into me.

"Your Aunt Cassie worries about you. I worry about you. You haven't answered your phone in days. Cassie said you haven't left the cottage. How do you feel? Have you taken your pills?"

My anger flashed, red and jagged. "Cassie told you about those?"

"It's okay, Maddie. She was just worried about you, and so am I."

"Yes, Doctor," I spat out the words. They tasted bitter in my mouth. "I see. You don't have to pretend, you know. I thought you were interested in me, in who I am. I'm a fool. Just stay away from me, Dr. Manning. I can manage on my own," I said, pulling my robe tighter around me.

"Maddie, listen!" Clayton searched my eyes, willing me to believe him. "You're a beautiful young woman. You must know I like you a lot."

"I'm not. You don't."

"Yes, I do!" he said, his eyes flashing. He dropped my hands. "I'm not here as your doctor. I'm here as someone who cares, dammit!" He stood over me, cupped my face with his hands and kissed me on the mouth, passionate and hungry; The most natural thing in the world. My whole being blazed into life at his touch. Then he broke away, covering his face with his hands.

"Sorry, Maddie," he moaned through his fingers. "I didn't mean to do that—not with you so vulnerable. What you must think of me?"

"It's okay," I said, catching my breath. "I know it sounds crazy, but—I've wanted to do that since we first met."

Clayton sat down in an armchair by the window. A safe distance away. We both sat in silence for a while, listening to the wind whistle around the roof of the cottage. I stared out the window at the swaying trees, feeling fragile. I was like those trees, battered by the storm of conflicting emotions in my heart; by feelings and events over which I had no control.

"Okay, so… now what?" he looked at the floorboards, waiting for me to take the lead.

I turned away, holding my arms to my chest. "This complicates things. I'm having a hard time… my diagnosis, John dying, finding out there's a murderer out there, and then… I always fall too hard, too fast! Then I find my heart in little pieces, you know? You're older than me, too, Clayton. Not that that's a bad thing," I blurted as Clayton rose to protest. "It just makes me feel a little inexperienced, vulnerable even."

"I've only had one serious relationship before," said Clayton, sitting back down. "I'm not as experienced as you think."

"It's not just that," I said, feeling the heat rise in my cheeks. "You don't understand: I mean, I'm waiting… for the right guy. For marriage, you know?"

I put my head down against the couch cushions, wishing I could crawl underneath, unseen. I didn't dare look at him. This was tricky ground for me: chastity before marriage was a belief I held sacred, ingrained from my Catholic upbringing. Now that I was struggling to keep my moods stable, it was even more important to control my passions.

"Oh, I see." He was silent for a minute. If he was surprised, he didn't show it. "And you don't think I'm the marrying type?" His eyes challenged me. Intelligent and probing, they saw through my defences.

I took a deep breath and drew my robe tighter around me. "Look, whatever this is between us, let's just take it slow, okay? Right now, I need to think about what to do."

"You're not going back, are you?"

"To the city? Not a chance. What I meant was, I keep thinking about what to do about Uncle John. I'm sure someone murdered him, Clayton. It's the only thing that makes sense. And not by Aunt Cassie, but by someone who wants to frame her. I've got to find out who did that to him."

"Maddie, that's what the police are for. If it's murder, they will find the killer. You need to focus on yourself, right now. I'm not sure it's healthy for you to be here anymore, is there somewhere else you can go?"

I stared at him. "Why? This is where I need to be! I need to grieve with my Aunt Cassie. And I need to be here to figure out what happened to Uncle John. You don't have to help me. But you can't stop me!"

"All right, Maddie. But from what your Aunt Cassie has been telling me, you're sinking into depression again, and I won't let that happen."

"I'm fine, Clayton. Well, no I'm not: I'm grieving. And you're right, I'm fighting depression. But at least I'm fighting. Besides, putting my mind to work on finding Uncle John's killer might be the perfect distraction."

Clayton sighed. "If you do find out anything important, Rebecca needs to know right away, okay?"

"Okay," I said, feeling lighter inside. Then I wondered again why he and Detective Trent were on a first-name basis and whether I needed to feel jealous. I chased this thought away. No more negative thoughts.

I saw Clayton studying me, his brows furrowed.

"Are you sure you're feeling all right?" he asked.

"Well, I'm tired. I feel heavy and slow. It's been two days since I took my pills. Because I was sleeping so much, I think. Anyway, I'm glad you're here."

Clayton leaned forward. "Me, too." Those blue eyes were a

magnet: with an effort, I tore my eyes away. I liked Clayton, and I liked the way I felt with him. But I had to be careful: I was way too vulnerable.

"I think you should get out of here, Maddie," Clayton said, rising from his chair. "How about coming with me to town? We can get a bite to eat at the cafe, and then I'll show you around my office. It's closed on Mondays."

I hesitated. I knew Clayton was right—I needed to get out. It wasn't a good idea to be alone, to wallow in my grief. I also wanted an opportunity to investigate my Uncle John's death and I couldn't do that in a cabin in the woods. Yet, I knew that I was falling for Clayton—hard and fast. I had fallen hard and fast before, and it led to heartache. Was I strong enough to take this slow? I hoped so.

"All right, Clayton," I said, smiling. "Give me a minute to get ready and I'll come with you. Just as friends for now, though, okay?"

"Sounds like a plan," said Clayton, his blue eyes flashing innocence. I looked away. Those innocent eyes didn't fool me—not for one minute. I would need to be careful.

CHAPTER ELEVEN

At Wren's Bakery and Grill, there were many customers chatting at large oak tables eating various baked delights. That cheerful chatter dwindled away as soon as Clayton and I walked into the restaurant.

"Is something wrong? Do I look funny?" I whispered to Clayton, and he laughed.

"You're the new kid in town, remember? I hate to break it to you, but you'll be under a microscope for a while. And now that you're out with me, people will talk."

We stood in the doorway for a moment looking around at the place. I liked it. It had an old oak counter, and lots of antique baking implements hung on the walls. There were also paintings. I recognized the unique style of at least one artist—Tuppence Millard. This piece had a forest landscape. All the trees bent and swayed in a communal dance, while points of light and energy floated under and around their leaves.

"Oh, she's so imaginative!" I breathed.

"Who?" Clayton asked, looking puzzled.

"Tuppence Millard. She's—"

Our server interrupted us, leading the way to a window-seat in the corner. There was a nice view of the main street and the forested hills beyond. Distracted by the view, it took me a moment to recognize our server as the girl from the dinner party—Tuppence's daughter, Alvira Minton. She sure recognized me, though.

"So, what's the scoop at Green Briar, eh?" she asked, sitting down beside Clayton and leaning in like a fellow conspirator.

"There is no 'scoop,' Alvira," said Clayton cooly. "The police are investigating and haven't come up with anything yet."

"Come on. You can give me more than that. I was there, remember? I saw Cassie bring John the cup of tea."

She had my full attention now. "What did you see?" I asked, studying her.

"I saw her bring the cup and set it down on the table in front of him. It's a tall mug, you know? Not like a tiny teacup and saucer or anything. More like a travel mug." Alvira's eyes danced at the drama.

I leaned forward. "Did you see John take a sip of it right away? I mean, could anyone have slipped anything in his drink after Cassie set down the mug?"

Alvira shook her head. "Nope. He drank it right away. He even remarked about how good it tasted."

My heart sank. That didn't look good for Cassie. I turned to Clayton.

"Someone could have put something in the tea after that, couldn't they? If he just left it for a moment?"

Clayton thought about it. "Yes, that's possible, or there's another possibility," he said, his gaze sliding from me to the window. "Maybe the killer placed the leaves in the cup before Cassie took it into the kitchen. John always had that cup with him, as I remember, and he was always getting a top-up."

I nodded. "If he left the cup for a moment, to go to the washroom even, someone in the room could have doctored it.

There were many people around, talking and listening to the music."

I thought about that night, replaying it over and over in my mind, but from a different point of view. "And he had that kind of mug that has a French press in it, so you can't see the loose leaves!"

"That's right!" said Alvira, bubbling with excitement. "He even brought it to the cafe, and we filled it up for him here. Sometimes it was coffee, but most often it was tea. He asked for lemon ginger… or sometimes chai or mint." We three sat for a moment, thinking about this. Then Clayton cleared his throat.

"Alvira, I don't suppose you could take our order now?" He asked. "We've got to get going soon."

I hid a smile. I didn't think Clayton meant to sound so rude. I was thankful Alvira didn't seem to take it that way.

"Sure," she said, jumping up. "What do you guys want?"

I ordered an espresso with a slice of lemon pie, and Clayton ordered a black Americano with a pumpkin spice muffin. We waited until Alvira had left to resume our conversation.

"So, you like art," said Clayton smiling. He noticed that my gaze kept reverting to the Millard painting.

"Yes," I admitted, smiling. "Very much. I adore landscapes, like that one. I had a great conversation with Tuppence about it at the dinner party. She paints, and I write poetry. We both agreed that poetry and visual art are very similar."

"I can see that," said Clayton, nodding. "A visual artist paints with physical mediums and the poet paints with words."

"Yes, and not only that, the two art forms are all about expressing raw emotion. I guess we could also put music in that category, except that it is less about creating an image and more about the feeling evoked."

Clayton nodded, and we fell silent, studying the forest

painting until Alvira arrived at our table with our order. She set two cups of steaming coffee in front of us, in large artisan mugs. Mine looked like an owl. Clayton had a bear. The pie and muffin were on matching artisan plates.

"Alvira, wait!" I said as she turned to leave.

"What's up? Did I get something wrong?" she asked, scanning the table.

"Oh no, everything looks great. I just wondered about the night John died, did you see anyone talking to him?" Alvira thought for a minute.

"Well, I saw Cassie. And my Mom came over to say 'hi.' And there was George. They were arguing—but that wasn't unusual for them. And I also saw Alex and Randy both talking to him at different times. So, I guess everyone spoke to him at least once. Even you, Dr. Manning."

"Why did George often argue with John?" I asked, my curiosity growing.

"Well, George's family used to hunt on the Jones' land — in the woods, at the back of the house. Then one year someone got hurt. I understood that John wanted nothing to do with hunting after that. But George thought that was taking it too far. He wanted to see the Hunt Club brought back to its former glory."

"Thanks, Alvira. I'd better let you get back to your other customers. I enjoyed talking to you, though," I said, smiling.

"Yeah, same. Maybe we could get together sometime and hang out?"

"Yeah, sure."

Alvira smiled at me, this time looking shy and vulnerable. This surprised me—I hadn't seen that side of her before. In that moment I realized Alvira needed a friend as much as I did. Maybe there weren't a lot of young people our age in a small town like this.

Clayton went up to the counter to pay our bill and came back with a wrapped package tucked under his arm.

"What's that?" I asked.

"A present for you," he said, smiling.

"For me? What is it?" I asked, straining to see.

Clayton laughed. "When we get back to the car, you can open it."

Sitting in the front seat of his car I tore open the package. I suspected I knew what it was, and I was right: It was the Tuppence Millard painting I had liked so much, the one with the forest.

"Thank you. So much!" I breathed, looking at the dancing trees again, this time up close.

"It's worth it—to see you so happy," said Clayton, and he touched my hand. I took his hand in mine, a strong but gentle hand, used for healing.

"Clayton, do you think George could have had anything to do with John's death?" His left hand on the steering wheel tightened.

"No. I don't. George is a good man, Maddie."

"It's hard to think of anyone as a killer, though, isn't it? You see perpetrators on the news being hauled away to jail, and their neighbors say: 'He seemed like such a nice man!' One never knows! Plus, George is a hunter. Doesn't that make him a little more conditioned to death?"

Clayton glanced at me with a wry expression. "Doctors and nurses see death often. Do you feel any more conditioned to death?"

I saw his point. "No, I guess not."

He took his hand away from mine to steer a sharp corner. "Look, I know George. He may like to hunt, but he has the highest respect for life. George is part Algonkian and feels the greatest affinity for nature. Before and after every animal he kills, he prays—thanking the creature for giving its life."

"That's admirable. I'd like to know more about the Hunt Club, though."

"George would be glad to fill you in, I'm sure. You should stop in at the Buck and Bullet sometime." Clayton pulled the car into a paved circular driveway. When he had parked, he turned to me, smiling. "Now, let me show you around my place."

The doctor's office was right beside his home, just on the edge of town. His house was an old brick century home, landscaped with meticulous detail. The office was newer, a little brick building. Clayton showed me around the office, and it impressed me. It was neat and sanitized like all medical buildings, but it had character. There was a lot of wood on the walls in the waiting room, burnished and glowing. Large windows framed a view to the garden, where there were small statues of woodland creatures, grey stone pavers, and coniferous bushes. There were a few paintings on the walls, (a little too abstract for my taste but with lovely colors and patterns) and the reception desk was a beautiful rich mahogany.

It surprised me to see he had a lot of the state-of-the-art equipment like an x-ray machine, most often reserved for hospitals. I supposed that a doctor's office in a remote town like Kenowa would need to be self-contained.

"Well, what do you think?" Clayton asked with a note of pride in his voice.

"It's impressive. I like the feel of the place—not too clinical. You know what I mean?"

"I do. It's a small-town practice, and I want my patients to feel comfortable. All it's missing is you, here, working alongside me every day."

Clayton's smile was hypnotic. I sucked in my breath. "Clayton, I…"

"Sh-sh-sh. Say nothing yet. Just think about it, okay?" He took my hands in his. "I wasn't kidding about needing a good nurse practitioner. My practice is growing, I need the help. Just consider it, okay?"

He pulled me close, and before I knew it, we were melting together, his mouth on mine. I struggled to come up for air.

"Hey, this isn't fair. It's so hard to say no to you! Just give me a little while, okay? A few weeks to get on my feet. Please."

Clayton smoothed my hair and I rested my head on his chest, feeling his heart beating fast and listening to him breathe.

"Okay," he whispered. "I'm sorry. I can't help it—you're magnetic." He kissed the top of my head. "I've got to go away for a while, anyway. Just for a week. There's a medical conference in British Columbia. I'll be giving a talk on some of my research. I have someone filling in for me here while I'm gone. When I get back, we'll talk about this again, okay?"

I nodded, already feeling a sense of loss. He lifted my chin to look into my eyes. "Be careful when investigating your Uncle John's death. Don't be risky. And Maddie, unless there's hard proof to the contrary, consider that it could still be suicide, okay? Even if it's hard to accept."

"Okay," I said, but inside I knew that wasn't an option. I was determined to find John's killer.

"Do you want to see the house?" Clayton asked. I hesitated, then shook my head. "Not today. Please take me back to Green Briar,"

This was madness: How could I feel this way about someone I had just met? What did I know about the real Clayton Manning? After what had happened with Uncle John, I wasn't sure I could trust anyone. A few days alone to think would give me a clearer head.

CHAPTER TWELVE

I hung the Millard painting in the guest cottage over the table. It was a good temporary home for it, and I could see it from the couch. I sat staring at it, missing Clayton and imagining my spirit escaping into that surreal forest, one with the dancing trees, their energy and color. The familiar melancholy was seeping into my soul and I began to write poetry again. I hadn't done that since my breakdown.

Branched hands
Embrace warm sky.
Leaves float soundless, down, seeking asylum.
The coldest night beneath me cradles secrets…
Become questions breathing secrets into nuggets.
Become sirens in my ear, whispering:
Truth is bare earth, caught alive.

The phone rang. It was Thalia Bateman. She wondered if I would like to visit her at the Bed and Breakfast and perhaps drop off a book Cassie had told her about. Not a bad idea, I thought. I liked Mrs. Bateman. I remembered her as a generous and kind woman, who used to give many sweet treats to me and Alex and

Randy when we were kids. It would give me a chance to talk to Mrs. Bateman about her sons. I didn't think either of them would poison John, but I wanted to rule everyone out. Besides, maybe she could tell me more about George Riddleman and the Hunt Club.

I drove the Nissan in silence, watching the wall of trees on either side of the road appear and disappear in the twists and turns. The car zipped up and down hills and through the forest giving my stomach a workout and my mind a thrill. Before hitting the town and just on the edge of Crowe Lake was a dirt road and a sign for Bateman's Bed and Breakfast. I figured I could stop in here for a visit and then pick up a few things for Aunt Cassie in town. Aunt Cassie had been sleeping late these days, so I could be back before she missed me too much. I had been spending a lot of time with her because I knew she didn't want to be alone.

I pulled into the driveway of the Bed and Breakfast and marvelled at how cute and quaint the place was. It was a lovely wood and glass structure with a large deck that went all the way around the house. Thalia Bateman had done an excellent job with the little garden and hanging baskets. The place was bright and welcoming. I loved that the house backed on to Crowe Lake.

I stepped onto the porch and rang the doorbell. Thalia Bateman came to the door appearing out of breath. I smiled at the big olive-skinned woman with the frizzy hair.

"Don't just stand there, honey, come on in!" She wrapped me in a big mama-bear hug and almost knocked me off my feet.

Thalia ushered me into her beautiful home. We walked into a large living area with oversized armchairs, low, wide coffee tables, and a window that overlooked Crowe Lake.

"It's a shame it's getting too cold to sit out on the deck. I remember Cassie telling me about how much you loved nature when you were little."

"Oh, yeah, I'm sure she's told you that favorite story of hers, about the four-year-old me putting dirt and plants on the stairs of my old house."

"Yes," said Thalia laughing. "She asked you what in the world you were doing, and you said you wanted to bring the outside in!"

I nodded and joined in her laughter. Mom said it often enough to make me feel like it was a memory, but I was too young to remember. As I stared around me, appreciating the potted plants around Thalia's living room, I realized I wasn't the only one who wanted to bring the "outside in."

"Well, I think that's just grand," said Thalia. "Cassie told me you used to write poetry about nature, too. Do you still?" Now I cringed.

"Sometimes," I admitted. "I guess I'm a closet-poet. It's a kind of therapy for me, I suppose. I don't write it for any other reason."

"I'd like to read some of your poetry sometime," Thalia gushed. "You know your Aunt Cassie's always bragging about you, don't you?"

I nodded. Aunt Cassie had always been my cheering section. I didn't always want the attention, though.

"I can email you a few poems, sometime, if you like," I said, fidgeting with the centerpiece on the coffee table. Most of my poetry was private and few people would ever read it. My poems were a way to help me sort through my emotions. I was thankful that no one had read any of my most recent, darker poems. Nor would they, if I could help it.

"Hello, I hear we have a poet in the house?" said a cheerful male voice entering the room. I looked up to see Alex's dark blue eyes laughing at me through a fringe of brown hair.

"You make it sound so glorious," I said wrinkling my nose. "It's not a big deal. I'm not published or anything."

"You don't have to be, to produce great art. You know, Vincent Van Gogh never sold a single painting in his lifetime."

"I've heard. I'm no Van Gogh, though."

"No, you're Maddie Malone," Alex challenged, grinning. He sat down on the couch beside me, a little too close.

I edged a little away from him, without making it too obvious. Why did I feel so shy and awkward? I'd known Alex since I was a kid.

"Poetry is when an emotion has found its thought, and the thought has found words... Robert Frost."

"You like poetry, then?" I asked, arching my brow.

"Why not?" said Alex with a smile. "Yes, I read poetry, along with a lot of other things. Surprised?"

"Yes, I'm surprised. I never saw you so much as open a book when we were kids. I was the one reading Shakespeare when I should have been doing chores."

Alex nodded. "Yep. It's true, but I had a secret: I liked to read, too. It just wasn't manly to show it, or so I thought. And I was a boy trying so hard to be the man of the house in my father's absence."

I thought about this. "So, you were a closet reader? And to think you made fun of me when I was practicing my lines for the play, Alice: Through the Looking Glass."

"Well, I had my reputation to protect," grinned Alex, with a crooked grin. Something in his expression made me catch my breath, delighted to recognize the boy I once knew and loved.

"Do you want something to drink, Maddie?" interrupted Thalia. I turned to her, startled, having forgotten she was there.

"No thanks," I said, shaking my head. "I have to get going soon. I have errands to run for Aunt Cassie."

"Oh, come now, honey. Try some of my nice home-made

mango-pineapple juice." Alex made a face behind her back. I giggled. I got the feeling that Alex had had more than his fill of Thalia's mango-pineapple juice.

"Well, I guess I'll have a glass, but I have to get going soon."

"Me, too," said Alex. "I've got things to do at Green Briar."

Thalia went into the kitchen to make the smoothies. I kept stealing glances at Alex only to find him staring at me with open curiosity.

"It's good to see you again, Maddie. I was hoping we'd have time to talk at Cassie's dinner party, but it didn't work out that way."

"Good to see you, too, Alex. I'm sorry we didn't meet up under better circumstances."

Alex nodded. "Me, too."

We lapsed into silence again. I shifted in my seat, searching for something to say. "Hey, it occurred to me on the way over here that Bateman is an Irish surname, isn't it? You look Irish."

"Yeah, 'cause I'm full of Blarney," Alex grinned.

"No, I think it's the dark hair and blue eyes," I said with a smile, tucking my hair behind my ears.

"You won't be moving out too soon, will you, Son?" asked Thalia poking her head out of the kitchen. "You know I'll miss you around here!"

Alex laughed. "Mom, Green Briar's only down the road. Most of my stuff's there already. I can move the rest of it in by the end of the week," said Alex. He walked over to her and put his arm around her.

"You can't get rid of me that easily, Mom. I'll still be here for you, anything you need, just say the word." Thalia gave him a mama bear hug.

"I'm confused," I said, frowning. "You're moving to Green Briar? I thought you were working on your master's degree?"

"Haven't you heard?" Thalia said, poking Alex in the ribs. "John left Green Briar to Alex. He inherits Green Briar along with Cassie. John and Cassie discussed it years ago. They didn't have any kids of their own, and John knew Alex would take good care of Green Briar and of Cassie."

"That's so wonderful!" I said smiling at them. Inside, I felt conflicted. It was important for Aunt Cassie to have help, but I hated to see Alex give up his dreams.

He shrugged his shoulders, looking a little embarrassed. "I guess so. I would rather have had John alive. The ranch isn't the same without him. And it's a lot of responsibility, which I'm not sure I'm ready for. I will give it a go, though, for Cassie's sake."

Alex took the smoothie his mother offered him and drank it down. "Thanks, Mom."

"Alex… you're not giving up on school to work the ranch though, are you?" I said.

Alex came back over to me. He must have seen the concern on my face because he put a comforting hand on my shoulder.

"It's okay, Maddie. I can work on my Master's thesis while I get the ranch underway. There's a lot of work to do there and we're not in the financial position right now to hire any help."

"Couldn't you sell your part of Green Briar, if you wanted to?" I asked.

"Maybe," he said, leaning up against the wall, hands in his pockets, jingling his keys. "I know it wasn't John's wish, though. I'll do my best to honor his wishes."

"What about Randy?" I asked. "Doesn't he get a part of the ranch, too?"

Alex looked troubled. "Well, no. He never cared to run things, you know? He's more into his zoology — he's focused on becoming a vet. I'll have plenty of work for him to do if he wants it. John knew I would take care of him. Always do."

At the same time Mrs. Bateman handed me a glass of the mango-pineapple juice. "Try this, Honey—made it myself with the juicer, you know? Alex, are you going out now?"

Alex kissed her cheek. "Yep. Gotta go, Mom. Gotta check on things at the ranch. I left Randy on his own." He turned to me. "See you at the ranch, Maddie."

"See you, Alex." I stared after him, feeling like I had missed something.

"Alex seems so grown-up. So responsible," I said after he had left. "You must be so proud of him, Thalia."

Thalia nodded. "I am. My boys are the best—I'd do anything for them."

I looked at her, thinking that was most likely true. Her boys were her life. According to Alex, her husband—their father—had left them when the boys were very young. For a moment, I wondered how she had felt about that. And how did she feel about John — did she care about him, or was he just an obstacle in the way of her son's success? Was she jealous of John's relationship with her sons? Just how much did she want Alex to inherit Green Briar?

My suspicious mind was ready to concoct all kinds of wild theories, but I knew I was being ridiculous. My thirst for justice was clouding my sensibilities. Thalia was a lovely person. I was sure it had been a relief to her to have had a positive male figure in her sons' lives.

"Thalia, this like sunshine in a glass, thank you!" I said taking a swig of the mango-pineapple. It was delicious. Thalia beamed.

"I knew you'd like it," she said, pouring herself a drink, too. "I learned how to mix fruits down on the island, you know? With a little coconut flesh."

Thalia was from Puerto Rico and was always eager to share her culture. "Thalia, how could you leave the warmth of Puerto

Rico to come to Canada, where it is so cold?" I asked her in wonder.

"Oh, honey, Canada is beautiful. Lots of beautiful people, too. And after I married, I had dual citizenship. I go down to stay with my sister for much of the winter, so I miss out on all this cold!"

"Ah," I said smiling. "You're one of those snowbirds from Ontario that travel somewhere warm in the winter. Are you leaving soon, then?"

"I'll go down later this year, I think. Maybe I'll wait until after Christmas so I can celebrate with the boys."

I savored my fruit smoothie and thought about Alex and the ranch. I wondered if he wanted to live the life of a farmer, or if he was just putting what he saw as his responsibility to John's memory ahead of his own desires. Wasn't he studying geology? Maybe his real dream was to be a geologist—or a poet. I smiled to myself.

"Well, I hate to drink and run, Thalia, but I have to get back to Aunt Cassie. I have a few things to pick up first."

"Okay, dear. So nice to see you though. Don't be a stranger." Thalia gave me another overwhelming hug.

I was about to leave when I remembered I wanted to ask about the Hunt Club.

"Thalia, you must know most of the people in Kenowa, right?"

"For sure," laughed Thalia. "I can't help myself. I like to talk, eh?"

"Do you know George Riddleman?"

"Sure I do, Honey. He's the owner of the Buck and Bullet."

"Well, do you know anything about the Hunt Club that he used to run on John's land?"

Thalia's friendly face clouded over. "No, nothing, honey. Sorry." She busied herself with clearing the dishes.

Well, that was strange, I thought. Was she being evasive?

Thalia saw me to the door. She gave me a quick squeeze.

"We must have a good heart-to-heart sometime, Maddie. Then you can tell me what's up with that handsome doctor of yours."

"Thalia!" I laughed. "He's not 'my' anything!"

"If you say so, dear," she said with a twinkle in her eye. "We'll catch up later."

I couldn't get out the door fast enough. I didn't want to talk about Clayton. It was too soon. I headed to my car. As I opened the door of my Nissan, I noticed something that made me do a double-take. Growing at the side of the house, were several white and pink oleander bushes.

CHAPTER THIRTEEN

A unt Cassie was just getting up when I came in.
  "Hi Aunt Cassie," I said, giving her a peck on the cheek. "Let me get you some brunch."

She looked exhausted. Her hair was a mess, though she had tried to throw it up in a bun, and there were dark rings around her eyes. It broke my heart to see her this way. She sank into a kitchen chair and looked at me with affection.

"Thank you, dear. I appreciate it. I should make it for you."

"You'll do no such thing. You need to rest. Besides," I kissed the top of her head, "I enjoy taking care of you. You took care of me all these years."

I'm not the world's most excellent cook, but I made us some passable eggs sunny side up, bacon, sausages, toast, and a pot of strong tea.

"There. A traditional English breakfast. Except, this is for lunch." I set it in front of her with a flourish. Aunt Cassie had come over to Canada when she was in her early twenties, but she still adhered to the English culture. I still remember her teaching me to make scones when I was twelve — the "proper British way" with loads of butter.

"Thank you, dear. It looks wonderful," Aunt Cassie gushed,

though she ate very little.

I attacked mine with obvious hunger. I had not been eating well the last few days. I couldn't think about food when there was so much else going on.

When we finished, I did the dishes, and we went to sit by the fire in the great room with another cup of tea.

"Look, it's snowing!" I cried with delight. Through the large windows, I could see fluffy white flakes floating through the sky.

"So it is," agreed Cassie, smiling.

"Look how it covers everything that's dirty and makes it pure and beautiful," I said, in the grip of a poetic spirit.

"How I wish that were true," said Cassie, resting her head on a cushion and gazing out at the white world.

I looked at her, feeling my initial happiness ebbing away. How old and frail she looked. The vibrant, capable woman I had seen when I had first arrived had transformed, almost overnight, into this pale echo of her former self. I would have given almost anything to bring a smile back to her face. She had always been so full of life, a constant inspiration to me. Now, it was my turn to help her.

"Aunt Cassie," I said, my mind churning, "What do you think happened to Uncle John?"

She looked at me with tired eyes and didn't answer for a moment. Then she said,

"I don't believe he killed himself, Maddie."

I nodded. "I don't either, but the alternative seems incredible. Who could have wanted to do this?"

She shook her head. "I've been asking myself the same thing. It doesn't seem possible that one of our friends would want to poison John. I keep thinking it must have been an accident."

"But the police don't think so," I said, frowning.

Cassie shook her head. "No. They think it was suicide. They

don't understand that John wouldn't do that. He was so full of life, you know? And he was a man of great faith. Life was precious to him, a divine gift."

"Was there anyone there that night—someone you might not know very well—who might have had a reason?"

Aunt Cassie pursed her lips. "I don't know. I can't think of anyone."

I tried a different approach. "Can you tell me about George Riddleman? Dr. Manning was telling me about the Hunt Club that John used to have on the ranch here, in the back acres of the forest."

Aunt Cassie raised her eyebrows. "Well, it was a real tragedy. George loves to hunt, and John used to love to hunt with him. Then one day there was a horrible accident. One hunter was shot and fell into a coma. Soon after, he died. After that, John wanted nothing to do with hunting."

"Was George upset about that?" I asked.

"He was, dear. He understood, though. He always respected John's opinion about things."

"But, Alvira said that sometimes George and John had heated arguments about the Hunt Club," I pressed.

Cassie's mouth became a hard line. "Now, she shouldn't be stirring up trouble like that. There were no hard feelings between John and George. They were best friends. Sometimes friends have disagreements. It means nothing. You can trust me on this."

I could tell I wouldn't get anywhere else on this subject.

"What about Alvira? What do you know about her?"

"She's a sweet kid. Overdramatic, though, if you know what I mean. And sometimes a know-it-all, too. She's the daughter of an old friend of mine. You met her, Tuppence Millard."

"Tuppence Millard!" I exclaimed. "She's the daughter of the

artist? But I thought her last name was different, Minton, wasn't it?."

"Yes, well, these are modern times aren't they, dear? You don't have to take your husband's last name anymore. In fact, I don't think Tuppence ever married Richard Minton, come to think of it. They lead separate lives now, anyway. Can't blame her. He was a drinker."

"But, they're so different, aren't they? I mean, Tuppence is so suave and confident and Alvira is so…," I searched for the right word, "So flighty. Like she's unsure of herself. I feel sorry for Alvira. She tries so hard to please. She's not like her mother at all."

"Mothers and daughters can be very different, though, can't they, honey? Look at you with your mother."

I smiled and nodded. "Yes, Mom's wonderful, but we don't always see eye to eye. She's all about propriety and socializing, and I'm more of a recluse."

"Not quite a recluse, dear, but I know what you mean. You're more introverted, that's for sure."

I stared out the window, thinking. The white flakes were still coming down, even heavier than before. It was beautiful, but Cassie was right. It seemed like it covered the world in white, making it pure, but the dirt and decay were still underneath. Feeling weary of it all, I sank into the cushioned armchair. Green Briar was my escape from death and sadness, but it had somehow found me, anyway. Now I must fight it or else find myself swept away.

Aunt Cassie's eyes were closed, and she was dozing by the fire. I got up and put a blanket around her. She wasn't sleeping well at night. Poor, dear Auntie, I thought.

I glimpsed movement outside. It was a tall figure in a bright orange winter jacket and blue tuque heading around the side of the building. Alex? Randy? What were they doing back here? They were heading to the front, where the barn was. I thought I might investigate. I didn't want to leave the warmth of the fire, but there were questions I had to ask the Bateman brothers. Alex and I had had little chance to talk earlier.

I grabbed my full-length coat and headed out the front door so I wouldn't wake Aunt Cassie. My boots crunched through the snow, which was now building up on the ground. I walked out past the paved drive to where there was a gravel path leading up to the barn on a hill. I met a very bundled Randy on the way.

"Hi, Randy! I'm going to check out the barn." He grunted and didn't look at me. We walked together in silence for a while before he said, "Did you know that cows have best friends?"

"Wow, no. Do you mean that they hang out together in the barn?"

"Well, only the sick cows or nursing mothers and their calves winter in the barn. The rest of the herd is too large. The beef cattle huddle together up the road at Uncle Regis's place. It's more sheltered over there. Uncle Regis doesn't use it anymore for farming, so he lets us. We store our hay there, too." He said all of this without expression, and without seeming to take a breath. Only once did he stop and look at me sideways. Then, he continued.

"Researchers from the University of British Columbia have found that cows with best friends are less stressed and smarter, too. More able to problem-solve than cows who grow up alone."

"Is that what you're studying in school, Randy?" I asked with interest. "I heard you were taking zoology."

"What I'm studying is more general than that. I'm taking courses for a pre-med degree. Eventually, I want to focus on animal behaviors. And I want to be a veterinarian. I get along with animals better than I do with people."

73

"Oh, I'm sure that's not true."

"Well, it is. I don't understand people at all. I understand animals. Many people with autism do. Animals are simpler. I can tell when they are friendly and want to hang around me. I can also tell when they want to be alone. People are harder to understand—they sound friendly but are not interested in what you have to say. People have so many thoughts and motivations underneath what they show on their face or with their hands."

I nodded. "Okay, I kind of get that. People can act one way and feel another. There are a lot of social rules, like not saying what you mean if it will hurt someone's feelings."

Randy nodded with enthusiasm. "Yes, that's it. So, if I'm boring you, just please tell me, and I'll stop talking, okay?"

"Sure. You're not boring me, though, Randy. I'm interested to know about animals and farming. I grew up in the city, and there's a lot I don't know. For instance, what is the difference between a cattle farm and a cattle ranch like this one?"

"Well, this is a ranch because it's bigger and we deal in cattle. There is no mixed farming here. We don't grow crops except some hay and corn to feed our cattle. In the spring we save some heifers for mating with the bulls and the rest we sell. We also don't do large-scale milk production, so it's not a dairy farm, either. Although, we have a pet cow who gives milk for just the family. Her name is Asha. Alex named her that because it means 'hope' in India."

"Is Randy talking your ear off?" Alex had turned up in the barn doorway. The snow-clouds darkened the sky, and he was in silhouette against the light in the barn.

"Not at all," I said smiling. "He's giving me some valuable information about farming."

"It's okay. I'm done talking now," said Randy. "I have to water the cows and calves. Anyway, Alex might want to talk to you.

He thinks you're pretty."

"Randy!" Alex laughed. "It's true, though. You are welcome to come to my barn anytime, Maddie. You're a darn sight prettier than Asha, here. Sorry, old girl." He patted the side of the cow, and she bent her head toward him. He scratched her ears with affection.

"Do you want to touch her? Here, on her nice soft nose."

"Oh, I don't know," I hesitated. I thought cows were nice, gentle animals, but I was a city girl, and they seemed so big.

Alex lifted my hand and placed it on the cow's long nose. Asha shook her nose and grunted. I giggled.

"Pleased to meet you, Miss Asha," I said smiling.

"Don't worry, Maddie, she's very gentle. Although, sometimes I need to let her know I'm 'boss cow' in the herd, if you know what I mean. And don't step around the back of her. She can't see you back there and can step on your feet."

"Right," I said, stepping around hay and manure.

"I'm done here, just let me rake up, and then I can walk back to the house with you. We didn't get to finish our discussion on poetry earlier," said Alex taking up a shovel.

"I'm looking forward to it," I said smiling. I watched as he tossed the manure into a wheelbarrow and then raked out the stall. Then he lay down the fresh bedding and led Asha back into the stall.

"There you go, old girl. Nice and clean now." Alex looked at me sideways, and I laughed. Something about him always made me want to laugh. He had a twinkle in his eye, a spark that didn't go out. It was sometimes hard to know if he was serious, or just teasing me. Either way, it felt good to be around him.

"Is Randy coming?" I asked as we left the barn together.

"He'll be along. He loves it out here. Takes his time."

"What do you think about this snow? Are the cows ready for

the winter?"

"It won't stay long. There are a few more mild days to come yet. But yes, we're getting ready. We've moved the other cows further down the road where they're more sheltered, and we have the forage and feedstuffs lined up."

We walked side by side into the white world. Alex looked around and raised his hands to the sky as though embracing it.

"I wonder if the snow loves the trees and fields, that it kisses them so gently... Lewis Carroll."

I burst out laughing and couldn't stop. My sides began to hurt; I was laughing so hard. Alex looked at me in amazement. "What? What's so funny?"

I shook my head and gasped for air. "You," I said. "You are so complex, you know? Mr. Farmer, Poet, Scientist! You surprise me, Alex!"

Alex bowed with a flourish. "Why, thank you. I try. I'm not a poet, though. I just love poetry. I wish I could write it like you."

"Oh, you flatter me. You don't even know if I'm any good."

"Okay, try me."

"What?"

"Come on. Let me hear some of your poetry."

I hesitated. "I can't. It's too personal, you know? I don't write it for anyone else. It's a kind of therapy for me."

"Please. I'll be gentle, I promise," Alex looked at me with pleading eyes and a sweet smile. I resisted an urge to brush that lock of brown hair out of his eyes. He looked so much like a boy asking for candy.

I shook my head smiling. "Sometime, I promise. You can read some of it, but don't say it out loud. It would kill me."

"Okay," Alex said brightly. "I'll hold you to that promise."

"So why are you working here at the farm? Why aren't you studying at school?"

Alex looked away. "People look at farming like it's only for the uneducated, you know? Like, if you're a farmer you must be illiterate, or simple. It's not true. It's a real business, and you need to be smart about it. And for me, there's something so poetic about working the land. I mean, it's raw, full of life. You're in the thing's heart. Life, I mean. What could be more real than muck and crops and animals who are content just to be? I enjoy my studies, and I enjoy being a rancher. Why should I give either of them up? I want the best of both worlds."

"But aren't you studying geology? How is it possible to apply that to farming, or to poetry?"

"The hidden connection is the land. Agro-geology is an important new science that's changing the way people farm and work with the land. It's important to know the mineral content of the soil and know what rocks are affecting drainage and plant growth. I'm interested in studying the direct application of rocks and minerals to farming operations for both crops and livestock."

"Wow. I would never have put the two disciplines together, but that's fascinating. Very impressive, Mr. Bateman!" Alex tipped his head in a mock bow. "Thank you, Miss Malone." He stopped walking and looked at me.

"You know, I enjoy talking to you, Maddie. And if I'm not mistaken, you enjoy talking to me, too. We should go out sometime. Would you like to go for a coffee or something?"

My heart stood still. I was not expecting this at all. Yet, I understood where it was coming from. I enjoyed being with Alex, too. We had a history together. I had to admit, I felt a growing affection for the farmer-poet, but I couldn't say it was physical. At least, not like with Clayton. It felt more like friends, and right now I needed a friend.

"I enjoy talking to you too, Alex, but I just started seeing someone." I avoided his gaze.

"It's Manning, isn't it," said Alex clenching his fists. "Maddie, that guy is bad news, and I'm not just saying that because I'm jealous as hell. He's a smooth operator and you should be careful."

"Alex, what are you talking about?" I said, taken aback.

"What I'm saying is; I don't trust him, Maddie. And you shouldn't either. He's done this before. I don't want to see you get hurt."

"Alex, I don't know what you're talking about," I said, my chest feeling tight. I couldn't seem to get enough air.

"That's not all, Maddie," Alex said looking at me, his blue eyes sombre. "Ask him about the malpractice suit ... and John's knee."

I shook my head. My stomach was in knots and there was a thick fog in my mind. I started to rush away, toward the house. Who did Alex Bateman think he was to tell me what to do? I wouldn't stand for this. No way.

"I'm just trying to protect you, Maddie!" Alex shouted after me. "Ask him what happened to his last nurse practitioner. Just ask him, Maddie!"

CHAPTER FOURTEEN

Alex and I avoided each other after that. This was difficult because Alex was always working at the ranch and he and Randy would drop in at the house for meals or to clean up. I was careful not to look at Alex when I passed him a cup of tea or some scrambled eggs.

Randy noticed nothing at all, but Aunt Cassie did. She approached me about it when I was sitting with her by the fire. I was writing poetry in one of my journals, feeling melancholic, and she was knitting scarves for everyone for Christmas.

"Is anything the matter, Maddie?" She asked, laying down her needles. "You've been so quiet around Alex. You haven't had a falling out, have you?"

"No, Aunt Cassie. Alex and I ... just don't see eye to eye."

"That's too bad, honey. He's such a nice boy. I had hoped you would get on well together; you were close friends when you were younger."

"Well, I do like him, Aunt Cassie. We just argued that's all."

"I see." Aunt Cassie was studying me, and to my horror, I blushed.

"Aunt Cassie, Alex told me to ask about John's knee and some malpractice suit. What did he mean by that?"

"Ah. I see." Aunt Cassie was silent for a moment, staring at the fire.

"Was that what you and Alex have been fighting about?"

I hesitated. "We haven't been fighting, Aunt Cassie. It's just that Alex thinks Dr. Manning is untrustworthy and I think—well, I think he's a very nice man."

"I see." Aunt Cassie gave me a knowing look. As usual, I think she saw things exactly as they were.

"Well, it was two years ago. John had had knee surgery and was in a lot of pain. He had his left kneecap replaced. Dr. Manning prescribed potent pain medication, you know? Turns out the stuff he was on was highly addictive. It wasn't Dr. Manning's fault. Not really. John was on the medication for a very long time, but he begged Dr. Manning to keep prescribing it. He was in pain, but he started to get a lot of side effects, and his personality changed while on the medicine."

She looked sad for a moment then fell silent. I knew she was thinking about Uncle John. I waited as she dabbed her eyes with her shawl, then continued.

"The situation became desperate with John and I panicked—Even threatened a malpractice suit, I'm ashamed to say. I just wanted him to listen to my concerns, to take action. Which he did, to his credit. He told me that the troublesome medication was now off the market and he would wean John off of it, and he did. I am still very much indebted to Dr. Manning for his care. He helped John through a difficult time."

"But Alex blames Dr. Manning for it. He seemed furious about the whole thing."

Cassie shrugged her shoulders. "I don't know what to tell you, my dear. In retrospect, I don't see how John's pain was Dr. Manning's fault. Or the side effects. I guess I wanted to blame him at first, too, but I came to understand it was just one of those unfortunate things out of Dr. Manning's control. That's part of the reason I invited him the other night. To let him know there were no hard feelings."

I didn't know what to think after that. I was angry at Alex for insinuating things that were untrue, but I also had a seed of doubt growing in the back of my mind that I couldn't yet admit to. If there was a germ of truth to Alex's accusations... And what about that other thing, about his being a smooth operator? I couldn't turn a blind eye. I wasn't about to get myself hurt. There had been enough pain in my life. I had to protect myself.

So, I did what I always did in these sorts of situations. It wasn't the best or smartest thing to do, but it was a way to deal with my emotions. I shut my feelings up in a big black box and hid the key somewhere in the back of my mind. Experience told me these feelings would fester and give way to an explosion later on, but I knew of no other way. I shut my writing journal with an air of finality.

"I'm feeling a little sluggish Aunt Cassie. I think I'll go out to the cottage for a nap. Are you okay here for a while?

"Of course, dear. You come and go as you please. Don't worry about me."

"Aunt Cassie," I asked as I stood up to go, "Have you heard anything more from the police about Uncle John?"

"Yes," she said, her lips forming a tight line. "The investigation's closed: they've ruled his death a suicide, though I can't see why. He would never have taken his own life."

I nodded and then reached over and took her hand. "I feel the same way. I will sort this out, Aunt Cassie. Don't worry." She smiled at me, but I could see that she had doubts. I didn't. I would find Uncle John's killer. And I wouldn't let my feelings get in the way.

CHAPTER FIFTEEN

I meandered back to the cottage, taking great breaths of the spicy Autumn air. The snow had all melted away now. We were back to milder temperatures for a while, before winter came for good. I enjoyed the sun on my face, streaming down through the glowing ceiling of red and gold leaves. Brown leaves crunched underfoot. There was no wind, and the air had a fantastic stillness to it that was a balm to my tumultuous soul.

Whenever I walked through the forest, I was almost whole again. Almost. When I closed my eyes, I still saw Clayton Manning's hypnotic blue ones. I let my mind wander, but I could hear Alex's voice, full of laughter and poetry. When I turned my eyes inward, I saw an empty void where a self-concept should be. Who was I? Who did I want to be? I wasn't Nurse Malone any longer. That woman had died with the birth of my illness. But I wasn't my illness. It couldn't define me. And I wouldn't let my emotions rule my life.

I heard a twig snap ahead on the path, and I froze. A beautiful doe stood in front of me, her large eyes staring wide. She stood for a moment, looking at me, poised to run. Then we both heard a shot in the distance, and she ran, skittering in a zigzagging kind of motion through a path in the forest.

I felt a foreboding so intense it took my breath away. Was there a hunter in John's forest? After he had broken up the Hunt Club? For a moment, it paralyzed me. Then, I gathered my courage and continued down the path to the cottage, my senses heightened. It was all I could do to keep from running, like the doe, from some invisible pursuer.

I reached the cottage out of breath and fumbled for my key. That's when I realized that the door was already open. Had I left it unlocked? I thought I had checked the handle before I left, but now I wasn't sure. I felt prickles up and down my spine.

"It's nothing to worry about. Get a grip, Maddie," I chided myself. I pushed the door, and it creaked open. The place was empty. I looked around for evidence of an intruder and found none. The only thing I wasn't sure about was the bedroom drawer: It was open a crack, and I couldn't remember if I had shut it or not.

I sat on the couch, staring out the window, wondering what on earth I should be doing. Was it safe to stay here? Should I go up to the house and ask Cassie for one of the spare rooms? Or should I tough it out? Maybe there was a simple explanation for the gunshot I had heard. Perhaps it wasn't on John's land? Maybe I had left the door unlocked myself, and now my mind was just weaving fantasies. If someone had been in here while I was away, it would have had to be someone with a key, anyway. Maybe Cassie had sent someone to see how I was doing.

"What do I do now?" I asked. As if in answer, I heard a sudden cry outside the window. My heart sped up to a dizzying speed as I saw two yellow eyes staring at me. It was a full minute before I realized the eyes belonged to a familiar silhouette: A cat was crying outside my window sill.

Relieved, I opened the window for my unexpected visitor.

"I am glad to see you," I told the ginger, black and white calico.

"I don't know where you came from, but I could use the company right now." The cat purred and rubbed against me. She allowed me to pick her up and bring her into the cottage.

"Oh, you're a good kitty! You can defend me from intruders, can't you? You know how to scratch, right?" I closed and locked the window, feeling somewhat better.

"Meow!" cried the cat, and I heard the hunger in her voice. I went to the fridge to get some milk.

"You must be hungry. I wonder what you do for food around here? Do you hunt mice, or do you belong to someone?" I observed the cat as I poured it a saucer of milk. I noticed she didn't have a collar.

"I'll call you Hope, like Alex's cow. You've brought me hope, little one. Hope that I can get through all this without going crazy!"

A shallow pan made an impromptu litter box, but I had to go outside to find something to fill it with. I found some sand and gravel from around the outside of the cottage and dug it up with a serving spoon, scooping it into the shallow pan.

"That'll do for your litter box. Now for some food and water." I rifled through the cottage cupboards until I found the perfect set of bowls. I filled one with water, and in the other one, I put the contents of a can of tuna. All set. I bolted the door again and lay back on the couch. I thought I should get ready for bed, but I was on edge and felt I had to be ready for anything.

After her meal of tuna, little Hope curled up beside me on the couch. It wasn't long before she was fast asleep. I nodded off for a few minutes, then woke with a rush of adrenaline, remembering the hunter and the unlocked door. It was dark outside now, too late to go back up to the house. I would have to wait until morning to talk to Aunt Cassie about the gunshot.

I sat up with care, trying not to wake Hope who was a warm

ball beside me on the couch. I would have to find out if she belonged to someone around the farm. I rather hoped she didn't. I liked cats, and I could use the company.

I got up and put the kettle on for a cup of tea. While I got the cup and a saucer ready, I thought about John's death for the thousandth time, trying to put together the pieces.

Who had a motive for John's murder, I asked myself? Because it was murder, I was certain. There were six of us who had the opportunity. Seven, if you included Cassie, but I wasn't about to include her. A real detective would, maybe, but not one who knew her as I knew her. She was the kindest person I knew and still very much in love with John after all these years.

So, excluding Cassie, there was Alex, Randy, George Riddleman, Thalia Bateman, Alvira and the artist, Tuppence Millard. Any one of them could have poisoned John's cup. Oh, and Clayton Manning. I couldn't leave him off the list, I thought, setting my mind like flint.

"Now, which one had the motive to kill him?" I asked Hope, whose ears perked up.

"Well, Alex stood to gain by his death. Not that I think he's a killer, mind you," I said pouring the water for my tea. "And Randy could have been jealous, I guess. He knew that John would leave his brother the ranch. That might have made him resentful. Still, I'm not sure I buy that either."

I put sugar and milk in my tea, saving some milk for Hope.

"Then there is George Riddleman. I'm sure that stopping the Hunt Club was a sour note for him but is it a good enough reason to murder? I think not. But why was he having these heated arguments with John? I must find out, maybe ask Alex or Aunt Cassie." I brought my tea over to the couch and pulled up the coffee table to set it on.

"Thalia could have killed him to help Alex get the ranch, I

suppose, but that seems a little silly. Alvira and Tuppence don't seem to have much connection to John, but I'll keep digging. Clayton." I stopped, feeling conflicted. "I'm not sure what reason Clayton would have had to kill John, but I can't leave him out of it."

I glanced over at the cat. She was looking at me sagely through two slits for eyes. "You've got it all figured out, don't you, Miss Hope! Well, I'm not as clever as you are, Pretty Kitty. I'll have to give it more thought. Right now, though, I want to forget all about it and catch up on my reading."

I grabbed a book I had left on the coffee table and put murder out of my mind. Soon I was fast asleep with Hope curled up beside me.

CHAPTER SIXTEEN

Aunt Cassie said that my cat was a barn cat, that she had belonged to my Uncle John.

"I'm sure she's feeling displaced now that John's gone," said Aunt Cassie. "If you want to keep her at the cottage, that's fine. You can keep each other company. We have other barn cats that can do the job of catching mice."

"I'd like that, Aunt Cassie," I said, giving her a peck on the cheek. "Thank you."

"Don't mention it. Cup of tea, dear? Eggs and sausage?"

"Yes, thank you, Aunt Cassie." It warmed my heart to see her looking better, bustling around the kitchen like it was her little kingdom again. The bags under her eyes had gone, and she looked like she had had some sleep. I was about to tell her so, but thought better of it. Let her grow stronger without calling attention to the fact. That's what I wanted for myself. I hated it when people said, "Oh, you're looking better," which just highlighted how I was looking horrible before. I didn't want to relive memories of my illness or the pain it caused. I knew, too, that just because Aunt Cassie was getting stronger again, it didn't mean that she wasn't still in pain. It would be a long, hard road.

I was sitting down to eat when Randy and Alex came in.

"Hi, boys, care for some breakfast?" Aunt Cassie smiled.

"Yes," said Randy, looking at the floor. "I'd love some, Cassie. Thanks!" said Alex smiling at her and sitting down right next to me. I was uncomfortable and a little annoyed.

"Hi, Maddie. How are you?" asked Alex looking at Aunt Cassie and winking.

I bristled. "Fine, thank-you," I said, looking down at my plate.

"I'll get your breakfast," said Aunt Cassie, hurrying out of the room.

"Are you talking to me now, or just being polite?" Alex brushed a strand of hair out of my eyes so I could no longer hide my expression. I glared at him and edged away.

"I'm still mad about what you said. You can't drag a person's name through the mud, just because you don't like him."

Alex pursed his lips, his sunny face clouding over. "Please don't be mad at me, Maddie. I can't help your feelings or change your mind. I just want you to go into this with your eyes open, you know?"

I had to smile. It was hard to stay mad at Alex. He was so very likeable. "Okay, Alex. Let's just forget about it."

"Sure. Friends?" asked Alex, extending his hand. I took it.

"Friends."

"I want you to know that I talked to Aunt Cassie about John's knee. She doesn't blame Clayton."

"You're talking about Dr. Manning?" asked Randy in surprise. "What are you mad about? Did he do something to you?"

"No, Randy! Dr. Manning and I are friends. Good friends. He wouldn't hurt me." Alex snorted. I threw him a withering look.

"But he might, you know," said Randy. "I mean, there was that official inquiry two years ago when he was under investigation. A patient claimed he prescribed a medication that she didn't need. And she wasn't the only one. And then that nice Nurse Wessel quit. Didn't give a reason, just left town."

My throat went dry. Somehow Randy's point of view had more weight. He always seemed so candid about things. It was in his nature. That was true for many of the people I had known with autism.

"Did anything come of the investigation?" I asked, trying to sound like I didn't care. Lord knows I was trying not to care.

"Nope. They cleared him. But it upset the town, you know? It was hard to trust him after that. I know several people who will travel an hour out of town to go to a doctor, just to avoid him."

"But if they cleared him of charges, then he's innocent, right?"

Randy shrugged. "Maybe. Or maybe they just didn't have enough evidence to ruin his career over it. Who knows?"

Aunt Cassie came back to the table carrying a tray of breakfast for Alex and Randy. I got up to clear the table.

"Maddie, are you planning to go out to town today?" Cassie asked.

"Well, I was thinking about a trip into town, just to explore the area. Why?"

"Oh, it's nothing, luv. Just if you can pick me up a bag of sugar and some nutmeg, I'd appreciate it. I wanted to bake some pumpkin spice muffins this afternoon."

"I will but, only if I can have some of those muffins," I said, smiling. Aunt Cassie laughed. Glad she's back to her baking, I thought. It was a good sign.

"If you wait a few minutes, I can come with you to show you around town," Alex offered.

I hesitated.

"I don't know."

"Come on," he pleaded. "What are friends for?" I had another flash memory of Alex as a boy, with the same charming smile, hands in his pockets and leaning against the white fence. How could I resist that boyish charm?

"Well, okay, sure. Why not?" I smiled, allowing myself to enjoy his company. I wasn't sure how I would do any snooping around with Alex's watchful eye on me, but I was glad of the companionship. It was a relief to have Alex beside me again.

CHAPTER SEVENTEEN

We took Alex's truck, a beat-up old Ford. It seemed everyone had a truck in Kenowa—a testament to how tricky the winters were for driving. I was sure the truck came in handy on the farm, too.

We drove in silence down the winding country road. It was a blustery day; the wind was blowing the dead leaves off the trees and across the road. I liked Fall days like these for their sense of foreboding and excitement, but I felt a pang of grief for the beautiful trees that would soon be barren and cold.

"Has anyone been hunting at Green Briar lately?" I asked Alex. I had decided not to talk about this during breakfast because I didn't want Aunt Cassie to worry.

Alex glanced over at me. "Not that I know of, why?"

"Well, I heard a shot yesterday, walking to the cottage. I saw a deer right in front of me, too, and it ran away when it heard the shot."

Alex was silent, his sunny face taking on a grave expression. It was so unlike him, so unnatural that I reached out and touched his arm, to console him somehow. He threw me a strange look, and I drew my hand away.

"Sorry. Just say something. Is there something wrong?"

Alex's brow smoothed, and I relaxed again. "No, it's fine. At least, it will be. There must have been a poacher at Green Briar, but I wouldn't worry too much about it. I'll take a walk around the forest tomorrow to look for signs of poaching. I might have to tell the police."

"Have you had poachers before?"

"Yes, a long time ago. I didn't think it was an issue any more. Some neighbors of ours used to hunt in our forests. They seemed to think it was okay since they'd been doing it for years before John took over or even noticed. I remember John having to get the police involved before they would take him at his word and stay off his land."

That made me think about the Hunt Club and George Riddleman.

"Okay but, Uncle John hunted himself, right?" I asked.

"Mm-hmm. But that was different. We controlled our little Hunt Club. I mean, it was John's land."

"We? Were you a member of the Hunt Club, too?" I asked, surprised.

"Why does that surprise you?" Alex looked amused.

"Oh, I don't know, maybe I don't expect poet-farmers to hunt. I've seen you care for the animals. I guess I didn't see you as the violent type."

It was Alex's turn to look surprised. "I'm not. But hunting isn't senseless violence, Maddie. For people in the country, it's an important skill. I love the animals. But I'm an animal, too, right? I need food as much as any other predator. I feel sorry when I sell my cows for meat, too. But it is necessary for my survival, for the survival of the farm. When I hunt, I'm not some big-game hunter just doing it for the sport."

"No, I guess not." I thought for a moment. "Who else was in the Hunt Club?"

"Well, it wasn't an organized thing. Whoever could go, would go. It was me, John, Randy, the brothers Matt and Derek, our friend Steve, George, and Spooky Joe. Oh, and sometimes Tuppence Millard."

"The artist?" I asked in amazement.

"Yeah, artists hunt too, you know. People from all walks of life. Maybe you'd like to try it sometime."

"Hmmm. No thanks. Not my thing. But, who was the one who got hurt? And who on earth is Spooky Joe?"

Alex laughed. I liked his laugh. It was natural, spontaneous and ready to burst out of him at a moment's notice. I reflected that maybe this was because Alex was usually happy. I envied him this.

"Joe McConnell is an old codger that lives in a shack in the bush. The town kids started calling him Spooky Joe because he lives by himself and scares them off his property when they come by to pick raspberries and go fishing in the Whispering Woods. He's a good old boy, though. He entertains us with lots of stories of his childhood in Scotland."

"Joe wasn't the one hurt, was he?"

"Oh no. It was Steve Braeman," said Alex, his smile gone. "Poor Steve."

"What happened?"

"Well, Randy, George, John and I were hunting mostly within sight of each other at the northeast end as we agreed. Steve had strayed too far to the south-east corner of the woods, out of our sight. He must have thought he saw a deer or moose and didn't think he had time to tell us. We each fired two or three shots at some wild turkey moving in the bush. Only, it wasn't a wild turkey. We found young Steve bleeding out on the forest floor. We got help, but a little too late. Steve slipped into a coma, and then a few days later, he died."

"But I don't understand how it could happen. I mean, you were all experienced hunters, right? And wouldn't he have been wearing one of those bright orange vests?"

Alex nodded. "It's a strange thing, but experienced hunters are more likely to mistake other things and people for prey. We have more of what's called a 'cognitive bias:' The brain sees what we want it to see. We can see even a hunter with an orange vest as a turkey or deer if that is what we are expecting."

I looked out the window, sad about this waste of life. The sky seemed sad too, crying big fat raindrops on the windshield.

We had reached the town, and I looked out at the quaint little shops. I had only been to the convenience store and Wren's Bakery and Grill. And Dr. Manning's office… But I forced myself not to think about that. There was some knot there in my mind and heart, and I would leave it alone for now.

"Where are we going first?" I asked, looking sideways at Alex. He smiled.

"It's a surprise." He drove a little past the stores and turned right down a side road that I hadn't noticed. In another moment, I beheld a river and then water rushing through an ancient-looking dam. There were walls along the river made of stone and concrete and benches to sit on to look at the water.

"The first stop is Crowe's Feet dam, which is on Crowe Lake. It is as old as the town, set up in 1866. You can see the date stamped into the concrete. The first settlers were always afraid of it. The logging company that built the first dam made it only 12 meters high out of wood timbers, but it held up the entire lake. Come on!"

Alex jumped out of the truck, and I followed, his enthusiasm catching.

"Alex, wait up!" I laughed. "What about the rain?" I ran after him to the water's edge. We were lucky the rain had slowed to a trickle, though the sky still threatened to pour.

"Hey, it's not wooden!" I pointed an accusing finger at the dam.

"Not anymore," said Alex. "They rebuilt it twice. But the original wooden dam worked—even though many of the villagers in Kenowa couldn't sleep at night thinking about it. They had people whose sole job it was to keep an eye on the dam and make sure there were no signs of leaking. It powered a grist mill and an electric light plant."

"How do you know all this?" I asked, laughing. "Now we can add Historian to your list of talents."

Alex shrugged. "I can't help it if my brain just soaks up facts,"

"Well, I am blessed to have a friend like you," I said smiling.

Alex looked away, toward the water. Then he recited a poem I had not heard before:

I will be the waves,
and you will be a strange shore.
I shall roll on and on and on,
and break upon your lap with
laughter. And no one in the world
will know where we both are.

Alex turned to me. "A quote from Rabindranath Tagore. He won the Pulitzer Prize for his poetry in 1913. His poetry is awesome: He gives a voice to my soul."

I looked out on the water and felt very fragile, knowing I was that strange shore, the stretch of land the waves could never quite reach.

"That's beautiful. Thank you, Alex," I breathed.

I studied Alex's face with its tender expression. I traced with my eyes his thoughtful chin, the dark brows above blue eyes, his brown hair, too long in the front, his chiseled cheekbones.

Someone could love him, I thought. Someone could love this man with a passion. He didn't have the suave manner or smooth grace of Clayton. But he was a man of different depths hidden behind a charming, boyish demeanor.

I untangled myself from these thoughts. Where would they get me? Into trouble.

CHAPTER EIGHTEEN

"So, what's next?" I asked Alex, feeling adventurous.

"Another surprise. Come with me."

We walked along the shores of Crowe lake. Soon the rain was falling in torrents, and I squealed and ran with Alex in the lead. The nearest cover was a long, low cedar building painted grey and white. A large orange sign proclaimed it to be "The Artist's Corner." That intrigued me. Sopping wet and laughing, Alex led me inside the building where I could dry off in the warmth.

We were in a room decorated with beautiful paintings, and when I saw the woman smiling at us and sitting on a black leather sofa, I knew where we were. We were in the studio of Tuppence Millard.

"I am graced with not one, but two lovers of art. How lovely of you to come and see me," smiled Tuppence. "Just in time for tea. It's jasmine green tea, I hope that's okay with you." She motioned to the tea set on a wide oak coffee table in front of her. We both nodded and sat down in black leather chairs opposite her.

"So, this is where you paint," I said looking around me, enthralled. There were so many beautiful forest paintings here, like the one I had at the guest cottage. I marvelled at the paintings of woodland animals, too, done in exquisite detail, and the wooden animal carvings on tables of different levels throughout the room.

"I didn't know you did carvings as well!" I exclaimed, jumping up to get a closer look. I liked one carving of a wolf, in particular. It had its eyes closed and was howling at the moon, or perhaps he howled in warning: "Stay away!"

"Yes, though they are not as good as your Uncle John's. He did some marvelous carvings over the years." Tuppence poured us some tea.

"Do you like my little wolf?" asked Tuppence, handing me a full cup.

"Very much. Is he for sale?"

"Well, my usual fee is fifty dollars or more per carving and I sell quite a few of them to tourists. But I will give him to you for free. It's my 'welcome to Kenowa' present for you."

"Thank you so much! But I want to pay for it. I insist. You need some recompense for your hours of hard work." Tuppence bowed. I gave her fifty dollars and tucked the beautiful wolf into my purse.

"Not fair," Alex pouted. "You like her better than me."

"Now, now, my dear boy. Let's not begrudge her this. Didn't I give you a rabbit last Christmas?"

"Yes, and I love it, too. Thank you."

"Don't mention it. Now, will that be one or two spoonfuls of sugar?"

"Two for me," said Alex. "Only one for me, thanks," I said, enjoying the warmth of the cup in my hands.

"I have a poem for you," said Alex, setting his cup down.

"Oh, I'm glad. What is it today?" Tuppence said, her violet eyes dancing through long black lashes. She tucked her grey-brown hair behind her ears and sat back on the couch; her head cocked to one side.

"Ok, see if you can guess the author of this one," said Alex with a mischievous smile. He cleared his throat.

In the foreground, we see time and life
swept in a race
toward the left-hand side of the picture
where shore meets the shore.
But that meeting place
isn't represented;
it doesn't occur on the canvas.

"Hmm. I like it, but I couldn't guess who wrote it," said Tuppence.

"It was part of a poem Ginsberg wrote to describe Cezanne's Ports."

"And you wanted us to guess that?" I said, incredulous. Alex, being Alex, just smiled.

"Do you know, there's an actual word for poets who write about painting. It's called 'ekphrasis.'" He turned to me. "Have you ever performed ekphrasis, my dear girl?"

I made a face. "Ugh! That sounds immoral. And, yes. I have."

"Let's hear it."

"No!"

"You promised!"

"No, I promised you could read it. That's different."

"Please?" Alex asked, putting his hands together in a pleading gesture.

I stared at him poised in hope and smiled. Tuppence nodded her encouragement. I drew in a deep breath thinking it might be my last.

Ochre and crimson chiseled on masses of blue,
Claw your way across the canvas, Autumn Tree!
From the wind and the brush, you won't escape,
Vagrant leaves smear color,
In an artist's game of Chance.

"Bravo!" said Alex clapping, his eyes shining. I felt my face grow hot.

"Excellent, my dear!" said Tuppence smiling bright.

"Thank you, now let me disappear under your bear-skin rug," I said, grinning. Tuppence laughed. "I know how you feel. I used to be that way with my first paintings. But believe me, it gets easier. It's never easy to open up a piece of your soul for others to see. But yours is a wonderful gift to give."

"Thanks," I said, with sudden shyness. I appreciated any encouragement from the talented Tuppence Millard.

Just then, we heard a crashing sound from outside.

"What was that?" I asked in a panic. Alex looked worried too. Tuppence shook her head smiling.

"It's the wind, my angels. You must excuse me a moment. It keeps knocking over our sign about the Christmas party."

"You're having a Christmas party?" I asked.

"The whole town is. At the town hall and playhouse. You'll come, won't you?"

"I'll try."

"Good. Now I'll just get that sign up and be back in a jiffy." Tuppence put on tall leather boots and grabbed an umbrella and the beautiful poncho I had seen before. Then she disappeared outside into the rain and wind.

I looked at Alex and grinned. "Time to explore," I said with glee. I liked nothing better than to look at beautiful things, and this gallery was full of them.

"Me, too." Alex jumped up to join me. "Look at that one over there, the waterfall in the dark forest. Gorgeous, isn't it?"

"Yes." I peered at it up close, drinking it in. Then I moved around the room to an open doorway.

"Is this her studio back here?" I wondered aloud. I walked in and encountered a room full of easels and half-finished paintings. I wandered over to the closest easel and saw something unexpected. My heart sped up.

"Alex, come here! Who do you think this is?"

"John," he finished, nodding. "An excellent likeness, too. Unusual for Tuppence: It's rare she does portraits." What was most disturbing of all was there was a slash across the canvas, possibly made by a knife? Alex and I looked at each other, perplexed. Then I noticed there was a photo lying against the easel. I picked it up and could see three young people smiling. One of them was John, years ago. One of them was Tuppence. I didn't know the other young man with them. Tuppence was looking at John and had her arm around him.

"She must have known John when she was young."

"Very well, too, by the looks of it," said Alex, looking at me with his brows raised.

"Who is the other young man?" Alex peered at the photo. "I'm not sure ... he looks familiar, but I don't know why." He shook his head returning the photo to the easel. And not a moment too soon. Tuppence burst into the room looking upset.

"What are you doing in here? You're not supposed to be here!" she yelled, her face turning red. I couldn't believe my ears. Tuppence had always seemed so kind and even-tempered. Alex and I hurried out of the room.

"I'm so sorry, Tuppence. We didn't know!" I said, leaving the room in haste. Tuppence shut the door behind us.

"I'm sorry too," she said, calming down. She took a deep breath and collapsed on the couch. "I didn't mean to go off the deep end. It's just—that's my private sanctuary, you know? I can't bear to let anyone look at my art until it's finished. Please forgive my outburst, I—I acted like a child. I don't know what came over me."

"I forgive you, dear Tuppence and I'll say no more about it if you pass me another one of those scones," said Alex eyeing the raspberry cheesecake ones.

"Dear boy." She handed me one too. "Maddie, you must allow an old artist her eccentricities."

At that moment the door burst open and Alvira rushed in, her hair in pigtails. Besides the pigtails, she wore a nose-ring which must be new, since I hadn't noticed it at the ill-fated dinner party.

"Mother, how could you!" she wailed, ignoring Alex and me.

"What is it, my love?

"Don't you sweet talk me!" Alvira stormed. "You know what's wrong, Mother. You put my name in as the elf again this year, didn't you! I told you I wouldn't do it!"

"Now dear, you know you're so good at it. The children love you playing the elf. Besides, Mayor Redfield was insistent, and I couldn't disappoint her. If you don't want to do it, tell her yourself."

Alvira considered this and calmed down enough to grab a tea biscuit. "Okay, I'll do it. But that means I get out of clean-up."

"My dear girl. Come and sit down and say hello to our guests." Alvira sat and looked at Alex and me with large, curious eyes.

"What are you two doing here together? Are you an item, now? I thought you were going out with the handsome doctor,

Maddie?"

My face grew hot, and I ducked my head down, avoiding her gaze.

"I'm just showing Maddie around the town, Alvira," said Alex in an even tone. "How are things going at Wren's?"

"Boring," Alvira pouted. "No juicy gossip to speak of. Hey, have you shown Maddie the playhouse yet? I bet Maddie would make a good elf!"

"What do you mean? What elf?" I asked, finding my voice again.

"It's for the Christmas play. Every year, no matter what play we put on, I play the naughty Elf who interrupts the play and tries to take over. I did it as a joke five years ago, and now everyone expects me to put in an appearance."

"That's awesome!" I said, laughing. "I love that! I didn't know you had a dramatic streak in you, Alvira. And they want you back in the same role? You should be flattered, you know. You must be a ham."

"Well," said Alvira softening. "I guess so. I used to like it, you know? But now it's a little boring."

"Why don't you mix up the act this year," said Alex, his chin resting in his hands. "Do something different, unexpected. Then maybe you'll enjoy it again."

"Yeah, okay. You may be right." Alvira thought about this, then jumped up. I realized Alvira was not the type to stay still for long.

"Well, I've got to get ready. I've got a shift at Wren's. I'm still planning on coming out to visit you sometime, though." She smiled at me. "It must bore you, being out at Green Briar all day. We should do something." Alvira left the gallery, slamming the door behind her.

"Sorry about that," said Tuppence sighing and shaking her head. "That girl is a going concern."

"We've got to get going now, too. Thanks so much for the tea, Tuppence," said Alex rising. I put my cup down and followed suit.

"I enjoyed our little visit. Come back again soon and maybe I'll have you try painting to go along with your poetry."

We smiled and thanked her and left "The Artist's Corner." The rain had stopped, but the clouds were still dark and threatening. I looked back at the cabin with mixed feelings. What hornet's nest had we stumbled into there? The little cabin held secrets to unravel.

CHAPTER NINETEEN

The Kenowa Village Playhouse wasn't open, but Alex showed me around the outside of the old building, decorated with white stucco siding and English Tudor style framing. It was a historical site, he explained, made into a courthouse in the year 1905, just after the town newspaper started.

"The plays are experimental, very avant garde. I like it when they put on Canadian playwrights, like Norm Foster, or else ones that have something to say. Or a good old British Comedy like Ray Cooney's 'Run for Your Wife.' Gotta love it."

"I like a town that has a theatre," I said, feeling giving in to a sudden surge of joy. Then I checked myself. Why was I so happy? After my manic episode I had learned to suspect any strong emotion, positive and negative. I realized I had forgotten to take my pills and had left them at Green Briar. I would have to be careful. Not that happiness itself was a problem—far from it. It was just that the higher my highs were; the lower my lows would be.

"I'm glad you like it," said Alex taking my arm. We were feeling more comfortable around each other again. I thought friendship with Alex could work.

"Would you mind if we stopped at the Buck and Bullet? George asked me to stop by when I was in town."

"Sure, no problem. Just don't forget we've got to get Aunt Cassie's sugar and cinnamon." I smiled, thinking of Aunt Cassie's pumpkin spice muffins.

"You're in a good mood, suddenly. What's up? Have you changed your mind about me?" Alex's eyes were bright and teasing.

"Alex, don't even go there," I groaned. But the smile remained on my face.

We got in the pickup truck, and Alex drove us down to the Buck and Bullet, on the main street in town. I was glad to have the chance to talk to George Riddleman. He was still high on my list of suspects because of his arguments with John.

We entered the shop, and I looked around me, surprised. I guess I expected a fishing and hunting store to be gruesome, with lots of weaponry and antlers on the walls. George's shop was cozy. There was a fireplace with a roaring fire—so very welcome on a cold rainy day. I was interested to see paintings and carvings of wild animals—some of Tuppence Millard's artistry, I guessed. There were paintings of other local artists, too. Some of them were pretty professional looking. All of them featured beautiful woodland animals; bears, deer, raccoons, and wolves.

George Riddleman sat in a low-backed chair whittling wood. There were dreamcatchers for sale around his desk, their feathers moving with the fan from the fire. He also had beaded moccasins and quill necklaces for sale. I reached out to touch one of the dreamcatchers.

"You like those, eh?" George asked smiling. He did not look up from his carving.

"Yes, they're lovely," I said, looking at them close-up. "Don't they keep out bad dreams or something?"

"That's right," George nodded. "My people, the Algonquians, believed that the spiderwebs on the dreamcatchers would filter out the bad dreams brought by the wendigo, the evil forest spirits, and leave only the good dreams behind."

"I have one that George gave me a few years ago. It seems to be working since I haven't had a single nightmare for ages," said Alex with a smile.

"Take one, Miss Malone," said George, his eyes flickering upwards.

"Thank you, Mr. Riddleman. I will. Let me pay for it, though."

"No. This is a gift. I feel certain about this. A gift will make it more of a blessing." He lifted one off its hook and offered it to me. I took it into my hands with great care, though was not as delicate as I thought it would be. He gave me the most beautiful one, with yellow and blue beads setting off the colorful turkey quills.

"What did you want to see me about, old man?" asked Alex, warming his hands by the fire.

"You know I want to resume the hunt," said George, putting down his carving. "Business is fair, but I could use the extra meat for my family during the winter months. You know I hunt up at Spooky Joe's, but the hunting is not as good there as it is at Green Briar. You have the water there, to attract the deer. And the forest is thick, protecting them against the wolves."

Alex looked troubled. "I don't know, George. You know what John's wishes were. I don't have a problem with it, but it's not only my decision to make. I must ask Cassie."

"So, if Cassie agrees to it, it is okay with you?" John looked hopeful.

Alex shrugged. "Yeah, I guess so. Just let me talk to Cassie, okay?"

"Do you think it would help if I talked to her myself?" asked

George, looking thoughtful. "Cassie and I are old friends from high-school, you know? Or would that look insensitive right now?"

Alex shook his head. "No, you'd better let me do it. I'll let you know."

I cleared my throat. "George, if you don't mind my asking, what were you and John arguing about on the day that he died? Was it about hunting at Green Briar?"

George glanced at me this time straight in the eyes. "It wasn't. But I'd rather not talk about it, Miss. And I don't think that's any of your business."

"I'm sorry," I sputtered, "I didn't mean to offend. My curiosity sometimes gets me into trouble."

"No trouble," said the big man, shifting from one foot to the other. "I just would like to forget that day, you know? Remember the good times."

We said our goodbyes with haste. It was now November and starting to get dark early. We still needed to pick up Aunt Cassie's sugar and cinnamon. I thanked George again for the dreamcatcher and followed Alex into his pickup truck.

"What do you think about Tuppence Millard's painting of John?" I asked Alex when we were alone in his truck.

"I don't like it," said Alex, his jaw tight. He turned and looked at me.

"I never thought John's death was a suicide, did you?" he asked.

"Not at all," I said, holding his gaze. "In fact, I have been trying to find the killer on my own. I didn't tell you about it because, I wasn't sure I could trust you," I dropped my eyes. "I mean, you know, if this were a detective novel, you would be the prime suspect: you were the one who inherited the farm."

"And what makes you think you can trust me now?" Alex teased.

"Hmm. I don't know. Maybe I can't. Maybe I'm fooled by your charming personality."

Alex's smile glowed. "So, you think I have a charming personality?" I poked him in the ribs.

"Okay, on a serious note, let's get together and talk about this sometime," I said. "Maybe if we put our heads together, we'll come up with something. I just can't let it go."

"Good. I can't either."

On our way home I was silent, thinking about the day. It had been fun, riding around with Alex looking at places I hadn't known about, like The Artist's Corner. I looked over at him and studied him in silhouette. He was also deep in thought. I was glad to know this poet-farmer, I decided. And I was glad to have found an ally in solving John's murder.

Back in my little cottage in the woods, I surveyed my little domain with great satisfaction. The beautiful picture by Tuppence was now hanging on the wall above the couch, the carving of the wolf was on the table by the window, and the dreamcatcher was hanging in the window. I considered putting it in the bedroom, its proper place, but it looked so good I wanted it in the open. Besides, I thought. I haven't been sleeping well the last few days, only catnaps on the couch. In either case, the window was the best place for it.

I sat down on the couch now, watching the sun go down through the trees. Hope curled up beside me, purring. The trees had lost a lot of their leaves, so the forest had given up its secrets. Everything was visible now. I saw a squirrel scurry by, big-bellied and ready for the coming winter. I could see the forest floor, covered in pale orange and brown leaves. It was not flat, but sloped up and down, here and there for miles. Most of all I enjoyed the orange and gold glow of sunlight through the silhouettes of sleeping trees, feeling its warmth on my skin. I knew it wouldn't be with me much longer. Soon the forest would grow dark and foreboding, and I would have to close the curtains and contain my growing fears.

Then a sound pierced the silence, a familiar sound, but still, one that caused my heart to race. I fumbled around my coat pocket for my cell. The screen was lit up, showing Clayton as the caller. I hesitated, then swiped up to take the call.

"Hello?"

"Maddie! What a gift to hear your voice! I'm still in B.C., at Fort St. John. They delayed my flight. A freak snowstorm— you should see it! Anyway, I won't be back for another day or two. Then we'll have some catching up to do." His voice oozed warmth and anticipation.

"Yeah," I squeaked.

"Maddie? Are you okay? You sound strange."

"I'm okay. I guess I'll see you later on then."

"Right. Are you sure you're okay?" Clayton sounded worried.

"I'm fine. I'll see you when you get back. Thanks for calling."

I ended the call. My heart was thumping like crazy. I willed my breathing to return to normal. This wasn't good, I told myself. I tried to analyze how I was feeling ... a whole mixture of competing emotions. It wasn't all romantic yearning, I realized: Fear was uppermost in the race. I was feeling very anxious about Clayton coming back. I almost dreaded seeing him again. Why? Was it all that stuff that Randy and Alex had talked about? I suspected that had a lot to do with it.

I got off the couch and closed the curtains. It was dark now. I shivered, and Hope stirred, her triangle cat-ears pricked up like question marks.

"What do I do, Hope?" I moaned. Hope listened, her ears pricked up.

"I've got myself into a real mess. You see this guy, this doctor has feelings for me. He seemed perfect, you know, at first." Hope meowed.

"I know. To be fair, I haven't been thinking straight. In fact, I haven't been thinking much at all. I should have been more careful. I can guard my heart better than that. Anyway, now I think I've got to push him away. I shouldn't have given him any hope, you know? Oh, sorry Hope. I don't mean you," I laughed. I sat back on the couch and stroked her soft fur. The purring resumed.

"And then, there's this poet-farmer guy ..." I breathed, not wanting to probe my emotions in that regard. I sighed. "Why on earth do I have emotions, anyway? They only cause trouble. I wish I was only logical, like Sherlock Holmes. Besides, I shouldn't get mixed up in any relationship, right now. I have a mystery to solve."

I looked skyward. "Come on, Uncle John. Help me find out who did this to you, okay? So Green Briar can get back to normal. And we can feel some closure. I want to find some justice for you and Aunt Cassie."

Hope was sleeping again, but I couldn't. I was wide awake, and no doubt would be for a long time. I had books to read in my suitcase—one delectable mystery novel by Louise Penny. I loved Inspector Gamache. Or I could read a Poirot by Agatha Christie. I've read all of them already but still love to read them again.

"I'll just get into a good book. Maybe it will help me get an idea about my mystery."

I got up and made some tea—Both Mom and Aunt Cassie had taught me that books and tea are inseparable. As I was pouring the steaming hot water into the china teapot, I thought about the Crowe's Feet Dam and The Artist's Corner. Then I thought about the painting of John in Tuppence's studio.

"It's so strange," I said to myself, covering the teapot with a tea cozy that Aunt Cassie had knitted for it. "What does it mean?"

Did Tuppence and John have some kind of romantic involvement with each other I wasn't aware of? I wasn't about to ask Aunt Cassie and dredge up a painful past. But if it was all those years ago, why was Tuppence painting a picture of him now? As a tribute to John's life, or did she still carry a flame for him? Could that flame have turned to hatred? The slash across his face said something about that. Could Tuppence have murdered John in a jealous rage? It made little sense, though. If she was obsessed with John, it would seem more likely that she would poison Aunt Cassie. Unless she meant the poison for Cassie? I dismissed this idea. Everyone knew about John's favorite travel mug. He carried it everywhere.

I poured the reddish-brown liquid into a white china cup. At one time, Tuppence must have loved John. At least, the picture showed they were close, on intimate terms. If Tuppence was the killer, though, that love must have at some point turned to hatred. What could have done that? I thought I could convince Aunt Cassie to invite Tuppence over for tea sometime. Then I could observe the two of them together, maybe find out more about their relationship and Tuppence's attitude toward John.

That settled, I took my cup of tea to the coffee table and then went to get my book. I would deal with Tuppence in the morning.

CHAPTER TWENTY

I woke up late the next morning. When I finally showed up at the ranch house for breakfast, I found Aunt Cassie, Alex, and George in a heated discussion.

"I am appalled you would even suggest such a thing!" said Aunt Cassie, her eyes fiery. "John's only been dead for a few weeks, and you already want to start up the Hunt Club? Shame on you!"

"It's my decision, too, Cassie, and you know that John was softening on the idea. Remember when he met with the rest of us at Wren's? He told us then that he was reconsidering." Alex kept his voice even. He was a natural peacemaker.

"Well, he may have said that to please you people, but I can tell you that wasn't what he felt in his heart! What happened to Steve broke him up, you understand? I know it turned him off hunting for good!" Cassie's eyes welled up with tears.

"We felt horrible about Steve, too, Cassie," said George quietly. "I won't do anything if you don't want me too. You know I have the greatest respect for you. I just want you to reconsider. Hunting has been part of my culture since the beginning. It is a way of life. I just want to feed my family, and you know that Green Briar was our traditional hunting ground long before the Joneses came to settle on it."

"Well, that may be, George Riddleman, but it's not hunting grounds now, it's my home," said Cassie sniffing. "But I guess things are changing around here no matter what I want." Cassie stifled a sob and left the room, leaving us in a cacophony of silent thoughts.

"You were right, Alex," sighed George, twisting the edge of his flannel shirt. "I shouldn't have come. I thought I could persuade her. We used to get on well, you know?"

"It's okay, George. I was glad you came. I wasn't looking forward to asking her on my own." Alex turned to me wearily.

"Hi Maddie, Cassie left a plate of breakfast for you, and there's tea in the pot, freshly made."

"Thanks," I said sitting down and reaching for the tea. "I guess it was good I slept in. I missed out on most of that discussion."

"Well, I'll see you two later," said George sighing. He shuffled out the room with a long face.

"Wait, George! I'll walk out with you," said Alex putting a hand on the big man's shoulder. He followed him out of the room.

I sipped my tea and ate my breakfast in silence. Then I walked into the great room and flopped down on a chair facing the large windows and the forest I loved. A movement out of the corner of my eye told me that Aunt Cassie was in her favorite chair. I turned around to look at her.

"I suppose you think I'm awful for resisting the Hunt Club," Cassie sniffed.

"Not at all, Aunt Cassie! I understand completely. It was a horrible thing to happen on your land."

"Yes, it was." She gazed out the window and into the forest, remembering that day.

"John agonized over it. It was his shot, you see. He and George shot at the same time, but it was John's shot that was ruled fatal. He was wracked with guilt for a long time after that. We tried to make it up to Steve's family, but really, what could make up for losing a brother and a son? Nothing."

"No, I understand that."

"Mrs. Braeman—Steve's mom—was never the same. She ended up in a nursing home, her mind quite gone. His dad died of a heart attack before that, much too young."

I shook my head. "How horrible."

"Yes," Aunt Cassie said sorrowfully. "So, you see why I find it hard to take all this talk about hunting again."

I nodded thoughtfully.

"Did you ever try hunting yourself, Aunt Cassie?"

Aunt Cassie shook her head. "No. I might have tried it… I considered it. Before the accident, that is. I like to fish sometimes. I used to be quite an able fisherwoman."

"Really?"

"Yes, I don't know why you're surprised. Except that you're a city girl, aren't you? Most girls growing up in the country have tried their hand at fishing."

"Maybe you could teach me sometime."

Aunt Cassie smiled and looked at me sideways. "Maybe Alex could teach you. Or that handsome Dr. Manning." I ignored the meaningful looks and considered this. I was sure Alex would teach me. Then I had a picture of the smooth, debonair Dr. Manning teaching me to fish. I laughed. Not in a million years.

"What's so funny, dear?" Aunt Cassie asked.

"Nothing, Aunt Cassie. What are you doing?" She took pieces of mismatched fabric in her lap and sewed them together at a rapid pace as we talked.

"I'm putting together a lap quilt. Would you like to try one?"

"Me? Oh, I'm not very—" Aunt Cassie handed me a few scraps and then dug around for a needle and thread.

"You can make a simple quilt just by sewing scraps of fabric together. There are different patterns you can follow. The one I'm making has what they call 'charm squares,' and you make them by arranging solids with prints." Aunt Cassie held up a beautiful lap quilt I had noticed hanging over the back of her chair. It had large squares made of four smaller squares of fabric, set on a white background. I looked at the pieces she had given me and decided I could at least make one of the four squares.

The two of us sewed companionably for a while in silence. It was a lot more fun than I had thought, and it took my mind off my troubles. I was almost finished sewing my group of four squares; my mind came around to Tuppence and the painting of John.

"Aunt Cassie, do you think we could invite Tuppence Millard over to tea? I enjoyed talking to her the other day. She gave both Alex and I tea with raspberry cheesecake scones, and I thought it would be nice to return the favor."

"Sure, I don't see why not," Aunt Cassie said brightly. "In fact, why don't we do it this afternoon? I'll take some of my baking out of the freezer. I think I have blueberry scones and shortbread for jam. I'll just phone her up and see what she's doing."

We packed up our sewing. An hour later, Aunt Cassie and I were busy setting the table and heating some scones and shortbread in the oven. A knock on the door signalled our guest had arrived. Aunt Cassie went to the door, and I waited and watched at the kitchen table.

"I'm so glad you came," said Aunt Cassie leading Tuppence to the table.

"It was good of you to ask me, Cassie." Tuppence put a hand on her hair, smoothing down the wisps that tried to escape the bun at the back of her head. "I wanted to come and see you after John died, but I thought I should give you some space."

"Well, I'll be honest with you, Tuppence. I'll never be quite the same." Cassie said, shaking her head.

"That's understandable, dear," said Tuppence. I studied her for any hint of falseness, but if she was insincere, her acting was impeccable.

"Let me pour your tea," I said, holding the ceramic teapot. "Do you take cream and sugar?"

"Oh yes please," said Tuppence rearranging her poncho and sitting in a seat next to me.

Just then Alex came into the kitchen and started washing his hands.

"Oh, hello ladies," he said with a bow. "Am I crashing your party?"

We laughed. "Come and join us, Alex," Aunt Tuppence said. "Take a break from your chores. How's that heifer that's been worrying you?"

"She's fine. I now know what her problem is—the vet says she's pregnant." Alex said this with a look of pride and happiness. Aunt Cassie squealed with delight and rubbed her hands together. "Oh, that's wonderful! I'm so glad it's not another illness. That's happy news! Did Dr. Moran check any of the other heifers?"

"Well, there didn't seem any reason to, yet. I'll keep an eye on them, though."

"I have something to tell you, Alex ... to tell George, too," said Aunt Cassie, suddenly serious.

"I've decided you can hunt again at Green Briar. I still have mixed feelings about it, but I've decided that George is right. Life does and must go on. Banning the hunt won't bring Steve Braeman back."

Alex smiled happily. "That is good news, Tuppence. Thank you. George will be so glad to hear about this."

He turned to Tuppence. "Would you want to join the hunt this year?"

"Green Briar has the best hunting land around... I might, as long as it's okay with Cassie," said Tuppence looking sombre.

"It's okay, Tuppence," said Cassie. "I've made my mind up about it. John can't care about it now."

"I meant to tell you, we enjoyed tea at your place the other day, Tuppence," Alex said smiling. "Maddie couldn't stop talking about it, could you, Maddie?"

I looked at him in surprise. "Ah, no, no I couldn't. Your artwork, Tuppence was impressive. I have one of your paintings at the cottage. Clay—someone bought it for me as a gift, because they knew I loved it." Alex looked at me closely. I lowered my eyes, feeling my face flush.

"I was interested in that one painting in your workshop," said Alex. "The one of John. When did you paint that?"

I just about choked on my tea. What was Alex playing at? I had wanted to ask that question too, but I wasn't planning to bring it up so bluntly, or so soon. My approach would have been more subtle. What would Aunt Cassie think? I watched Cassie and Tuppence closely.

Tuppence was calm and collected. Maybe she had expected us to ask about it after she had caught us looking at it in the studio.

"I painted it after John died," she said pleasantly. "I rarely do portraits, but I thought I would do this one as a tribute to a good man, a dear friend. I had planned to give it to Cassie as a surprise, but then you and Maddie stumbled onto it by accident."

"Oh, Tuppence, that's so beautiful. What a lovely, thoughtful gift!" said Cassie with tears in her eyes. She stood up. "My dearest friend, how can I ever thank you?" Tuppence stood up, too, and the two of them embraced. I wasn't convinced that Tuppence was innocent, but somehow, I still felt ashamed.

"I'm sorry," said Alex evenly, "I didn't mean to spoil the surprise. He glanced at me, his eyebrows arched. I shrugged my shoulders.

I cleared my throat. "Tuppence, the painting seemed quite damaged... Can you tell us how it happened? Will you have to do it over again?"

Tuppence's eyes narrowed and her face clouded over for just a second. It was enough for me to know there was a reason she wasn't prepared to give.

Then Tuppence smiled as though I had said something silly. "Oh my dears, it was the darnedest thing. I have these knives, you know, very sharp ones used to cut canvas. I set the painting on the worktable, you know, to look at some brushstrokes up close, to see if they needed correcting. I was cutting the canvas overtop of it and thought I was careful, but obviously, I wasn't careful enough."

"Oh, how awful!" said Aunt Cassie, looking pained. Alex and I exchanged meaningful looks. Aunt Cassie might accept this explanation, but we weren't buying it.

"Don't worry, Cassie. I have started another one. I expect to have it finished by Christmastime."

The tea went on nicely after that. Aunt Cassie and Tuppence seemed to be old friends, chatting about people they knew and goings-on in the town. It didn't seem like Aunt Cassie suspected anything wrong. Only Alex and I were silent during the rest of the visit.

Afterwards, I excused myself. I planned to go back to the cottage to clean up and maybe have a hot shower. It was drizzling outside, and I didn't feel like going out anywhere. A good book was calling my name.

Alex excused himself at the same time to go back to his chores. We both left Tuppence and Aunt Cassie together, deep in conversation about the outrageous prices at the convenience store and how wonderful it was that Abe Whitman's new log cabin was being raised on his once empty acreage of land.

Alex turned to me while I was getting ready to go back to the guest cottage. "Come up with me to the barn, Maddie," he said in a low voice. "Let's talk."

I hesitated. "Okay. My plans can wait."

We slipped outside and headed out together in the cold November rain.

CHAPTER TWENTY-ONE

Alex wrapped his old cow, Asha, in a woolen blanket for added warmth against the increasing cold. Then, the two of us sat down together on some bales of hay. It felt a little awkward being so close, but it was cold in the barn, and I was warm and comfortable at Alex's side. At least that's the excuse I was giving myself. Alex's eyes were bright.

"So, let's compare notes about John's death. We both agree that it was murder," he said, his brows drawn together.

"Yes, to my way of thinking, there's no question about it. We knew him better than anyone except Aunt Cassie, and she's not convinced its suicide either. Do you know why the police decided it was suicide?"

Alex nodded. "Yes, I think I do. You may not know this: John told no one except Cassie and me, but he had leukemia. The police figured he had taken the oleander to avoid further pain and stress, but I know that John was handling it well and he was in remission. If things were going well, why would he take his own life?"

I nodded, feeling my eyes moisten.

"Poor Uncle John," I said. "Why didn't he say anything?"

"Well, I suppose he didn't want to worry you or your mother.

Especially since it seemed he was in remission. He had to tell Randy and me because we worked with him and noticed he was getting weaker and short of breath all the time."

I shook my head. "Poor Aunt Cassie. They just got over the shock of having cancer, and then John dies in this way."

"I know," said Alex, patting my arm. His hand felt roughened from hard work but somehow also tender.

I smiled. "You know, I used to be a little jealous of you, growing up."

"Jealous of me? Why?" asked Alex in disbelief.

"Well, you were a boy and expected to help around the barn, you know. They expected me to help Aunt Cassie in the kitchen. I wanted to be looking after the animals with Uncle John."

"Why didn't you tell John or Cassie about it?" asked Alex, his brows raised. "They would have understood! Okay, I admit I was a little jealous of you, too. You got to hang out in the warm house and read. I love to read too, you know!"

I stole glances at Alex through lowered lashes. "So, we were more alike than I thought."

We were both silent for a moment, and I realized I was leaning a little on Alex's shoulder. My heart sped up a little. I straightened and edged away. What was wrong with me? Did I want to spoil a good friendship?

Alex didn't notice, or at least, he made it seem that way. "So, who do you think killed John?" he asked.

"Well, it's like this: eight people had the opportunity: you, me, Randy, Cassie, George, Alvira, Tuppence, your Mom, and Clayton."

"Right," Alex nodded. "But only a few of those had any motive to do so."

"You inherited the farm, so you are suspect number one," I said smiling.

"Okay, okay. Have it your way. You know I could never hurt John, though. Who's next?"

"George Riddleman."

"Why George?" asked Alex in surprise.

"Because he wanted the Hunt Club, and because he argued with John before he died."

Alex thought about this. "But, killing John wouldn't guarantee the Hunt Club would start up again."

"No, that's true. But what was he arguing about? It seems suspicious."

"Okay, we will have to find out about that. Who's next?"

"Tuppence. That painting was suspicious. The slash across John's face in the portrait was no accident. It was done on purpose and in anger."

"I agree. I'm not sure why, though. If she was obsessed with John, why kill him?"

"I don't know ... maybe because she didn't return his affections?"

"Hmm. In that case, you may be in trouble, Miss," said Alex looking at me with one eyebrow raised. I flushed and looked away.

"Now, now. None of that. We need to be serious detectives and focus on this case," I wagged a finger at him, and he laughed, lightening the mood.

Then Alex turned to me with a thoughtful expression.

"Okay, if you want serious, I'll give it to you. In all seriousness, I choose Clayton Manning as my number two suspect."

I groaned. "Alex."

"No, I mean it, Maddie. I know you can't see the devious side of him, but I can. I've been keeping tabs on him. Do you know where he's been the last week?"

"Yes," I said, exasperated. "He's been in Vancouver for a medical conference."

"Correct. But do you know what the conference was?"

I shook my head.

"The office secretary told me it was a symposium on the use of oleander in treating cancer patients."

"What?" My back stiffened.

Alex had a smug expression. "Looks suspicious, doesn't it? Maybe the good doctor was experimenting on John before he died, slipping him oleander in measured doses to see what it would do. Maybe he gave him an overdose by mistake."

"I don't believe it!" I said, but I didn't sound so sure of myself because I wasn't. I had to admit, that looked pretty incriminating.

"Well, I admit, it doesn't sound good," I said in a grudging voice. "Though, that we'd better rule out the other suspects, before coming to any conclusions."

"And we'll need hard proof before we accuse anyone for real," said Alex. I nodded.

I rose from the hay and brushed myself off, still stunned by Alex's news about Clayton. "Thanks for enlightening chat, Watson," I said smiling. "I'm going to the cottage now. We've got a lot to think about," I met Alex's eyes. I saw much more than I wanted to see. I wondered what he saw in my eyes.

"Okay, Sherlock." Alex grinned, rising to his feet. "We'll both do some sleuthing; then we'll meet again to discuss what we've found out."

I nodded. "I think I know who to talk to about Tuppence and George. I think I'll stop by Wren's tomorrow and talk to Alvira. That girl loves to gossip."

Alex nodded. "Maybe you should leave George to me. I think I can get him to talk when we are out hunting; he'll be glad Cassie's changed her mind."

"I know Clayton will be back soon from Vancouver." I broke off, feeling a wave of anxiety.

Alex put a hand on my shoulder. "Maddie, stay away from Manning, okay? At least until all this is settled. Promise me."

"Don't worry about me, Alex. I can look after myself," I said stiffly, walking away.

"I hope so, Maddie," he called after me as I made my way out through the barn. "Please be careful!"

CHAPTER TWENTY-TWO

I hurried through the forest, feeling the bite of the cold on my nose and cheeks. It was snowing, and a thin layer of white had collected on the branches of the trees. I loved the forest in this weather. I loved it in all weather. It breathed life into me, opened its branched arms to me as I brushed by. I observed everything—the air, the ground—everything around me draped in white, creating a stark contrast to the dark trunks of the trees and the long blue shadows. It also made the light streaming out of the cottage window appear brighter and more cheerful.

My breath caught in my throat as I realized the implications of that light, however. I had forgotten to lock the door that morning, but I was sure that the lights weren't on when I left. Was someone in my little cottage? I crept closer, my heart beating a mad rhythm in my chest. I intended to peer through the window, but as I drew closer, the front door opened revealing a tall, familiar silhouette.

"Clayton!" I cried. Adrenaline, like an electric shock, surged through me.

He smiled at me, leaning against the doorframe, looking so damned sure of himself.

"Surprised?" he said with amusement. "I was able to get a

return flight: It wasn't much of a stopover. I thought I would come straight here to surprise you."

"Well, I am surprised," I said, still keeping my distance. I wasn't prepared for this. I fought to keep myself steady.

"Come in, I have more surprises for you," Clayton said, leading the way.

I stared around the room, my eyes wide open. There were a dozen roses on the table by the window, and a bottle of red wine with two long-stemmed glasses. It was all too terribly romantic. Why had I told Alex I could handle myself? This would be much harder than I thought.

I sat down on the couch, contemplating my next move. I would have to tell him, I thought. I would have to be very straight, very firm. If I didn't look at him, if I didn't go too close, I could do this.

"Clayton," I began. "I have something to tell you. While you were away, I did some thinking, you know? I thought a lot about you, and well, the thing is, I hardly know you."

"I thought a lot about you too, Maddie," he said, smiling. He sat down beside me. I felt my resolve weaken as he put his hand on mine. "You're absolutely right. We don't know that much about each other. What I do know is, I'm crazy about you. So… let's get to know each other better."

He leaned toward me. I was aware of my breathing, shallow and quick. I could smell his spicy cologne. I felt dizzy. Then I remembered Alex's warning. This is crazy, I told myself. This man is dangerous. I inched away from him with the pretext of fixing my skirt.

I felt Clayton's gaze burning into me and I consciously avoided his eyes. I must not fall under their spell. "Clayton," I said, firmly. "What happened to your last Nurse Practitioner?"

He stiffened. "Who've you been talking to?"

"It doesn't matter," I said, keeping my voice cool. "Answer the question." I studied him through narrowed eyelids. He squirmed a little.

"Well, she left the practice because we had some differences." Did I glimpse some troubling emotion behind those blue eyes? An image of a spider flashed across my mind, a spider caught in its web.

"You might as well tell me everything. You know I'll find out anyway," I said, keeping my voice even.

He sighed, getting up from the couch to walk over to the window. "Okay, Maddie. But don't judge me harshly. It wasn't all my fault. I told you I had one serious relationship, right?" I nodded, biting my lip. Here it comes, I thought.

"Well, Deborah was the one. We had even talked about getting married. Then, I had some trouble. A patient I had been treating accused me of prescribing him a medication he didn't need. Things went downhill from there. There was a formal investigation." Clayton rose from the couch and began pacing the room.

"I spiralled into depression. I started drinking. Even, I'm ashamed to say, at work. I would come in still hammered from the night before. That didn't help with the investigation, or with my relationship, either. Deborah left me. And I don't blame her at all."

I wasn't shocked. It was what I had expected. I could imagine Clayton's position. One nasty report could destroy a career. Still, I needed to know the worst.

"So why did she leave town without a word to anyone?" I looked at him, screening his reaction. Did he seem a bit rattled? Even so, those intense blue eyes radiated sincerity. He took my trembling hands in his own.

"You need to trust me, Maddie. I would never hurt you."

I felt my throat constrict: That wasn't an answer. He was hiding something... Maybe Alex was right about him. Maybe the worst thing was true: Was he John's killer? I had to know.

I cleared my throat. "So, how was the symposium?"

Clayton shrugged. "It was informative, if boring, as they all are. They were talking about various treatments for cancer."

"Did you give your talk? What was it about?"

Clayton smiled at me, showing dazzling white teeth. "I did. It was okay, I guess. No one fell asleep, anyway. I talked about some new treatments I had tried and gave their success rates. You know I conducted a few studies in Toronto. I go down there a few times a year."

"That's great," I said, feeling anxiety rising in my chest. New treatments? Success rates? It was getting hard to breathe.

"What were the new treatments?"

He hedged a little. "Well ... extracts from different herbs, ingredients that could be reproduced in a lab."

Clayton observed me in silence for a moment.

"You're different, Maddie. What's happened? Is there something you're not telling me? Why are you grilling me like this?"

I couldn't look him in the eyes. "It's exactly what I said before. I feel things are moving too fast between us. We're not much more than strangers. As you say, I need to learn to trust you, you know? And trust takes time."

Clayton nodded. His brow was furrowed, deep in thought. I wondered if he would guess that I knew about the oleander.

I tried to keep the anxiety out of my voice. "Thank you so much for the roses, Clayton," I said. "They are beautiful." By this I hoped to dismiss him, but he sat there unmoving—staring at me as though I were a puzzle he intended to solve. I took a breath and tried again.

"Look, Clayton, what I've been trying to tell you is: I'm just not ready for this… relationship. I need more time to sort things out. It's—complicated."

After what seemed an eternity, he rose. "Okay, Maddie. If that's what you want." He bent over me and kissed my cheek, lingering just a little.

Before he opened the door to leave, Clayton looked back at me one more time. He still had that confident swagger, but his expression was more guarded.

"Can I call you later in the week?"

I hesitated, then nodded. A few minutes later he left, and I buried my head in the couch cushions, broken and confused.

CHAPTER TWENTY-THREE

I didn't sleep that night. The roses kept taunting me. The smell was overpowering, beautiful. As were the blooms, full and red and full of thorns. I paced the cottage like a tigress. Poor Hope didn't know what to think. Her mistress was losing her mind. She followed me with her eyes, uttering a "meow" to let me know she wasn't happy.

"Sorry, Hope. I am drowning right now. Drowning in emotion. Who does he think he is to blow in here like the west wind and think I will just bow to his charm?"

I grabbed my journal and started scribbling down phrases.

West Wind,
you have met your match
Send your boldest breezes
Unleash the dark cyclone twirling round
You won't dislodge me from the earth.
Oleander trees
grasping, groping, gulping
With hurricane force
They scrape, they fail.

I kept scribbling and scribbling, the dark matter in my soul oozing out like a cruel blood-letting. I kept trying to purge my mind of those evil blue eyes.

"He's mad. I'm mad. Oh, Hope, what do I do!" I tore out the journal pages and scrunched them up in little balls around the wood floor.

"He's experimenting with oleander. He knows I know it. What will he do now? He's a murderer, Hope. Or maybe not. Maybe it was just an accident, you know? Can I live with that?"

I opened the wine and poured myself a glass. I knew I shouldn't. I knew I was getting out of control. I knew mania's siren call, but I was on a railroad track, pummeled forward, I couldn't stop it.

Eyes haunted me. Clayton's hypnotic blue ones. Alex's storm-blue ones. Alex. He was right. He was right all along. I had been a fool.

I was sick of pacing. I needed to go for a real walk. I had my phone for light when I needed it. I opened the cottage door and headed outside.

"Sorry, Hope. You can't come. Stay and be safe," I said shutting the door. I was feeling quite tipsy, sometimes thrilled, sometimes hyper and irritable.

The moon shone down with a ghostly light. I shivered with anticipation as much as cold. I was one with the forest. At midnight. In moonlight. I was one of the forest creatures. I crept, I crawled, I sprinted like a stag.

I walked the forest path without difficulty. What would stop me? I belonged to this land. Finally, I came to the edge of the forest and had a decision to make. Should I keep going or turn back? I kept going. It was my secret thrill. Prowling around at midnight, a hidden, silent predator. Who could hurt me now? Not Clayton Manning. He was no match for me.

I walked around the ranch house. It was dark. No lights at

all. Aunt Cassie was sleeping peacefully. No poison for her. She was safe. I would protect her with my predatory night-walk. I would protect her with my great detective skills. It was my mission on earth.

I crept around the side of the house, my heart singing. I saw a light on in the barn. Did the cow need a light? Maybe Asha needed company. In the light, the ground whizzed by me too fast, and the world was spinning. How many glasses of wine did I drink?

I marched into the barn. A man was there, holding a weapon. I screamed. A hand clamped over my mouth.

"Maddie, Maddie stop! It's me! What the hell is wrong with you?" Alex took me in his arms, and I started sobbing.

"Alex, Alex. You were right. Dr. Manning is going to kill me!" I babbled.

"Calm down, Maddie. Calm down. Have you been drinking?"

I nodded. "He brought me wine. I had a couple of glasses."

Alex's face became stone. "I thought I saw Manning's car. He didn't hurt you, did he?" He shook me when I didn't answer. "If he hurt you, I will kill him. I will tear him apart with my bare hands. I'm strong enough, Maddie. I swear, I will."

I shook my head. "No, no, he didn't touch me. He just talked about his damn symposium. He told me he's been experimenting with new drugs. He as good as admitted it." I sobbed again, and Alex took me tenderly in his arms.

"You're so good to me Alex," I cried. "Thank you."

"It's okay, Maddie. Don't worry. I'm here." He cradled me and rocked me back and forth. He held me close, and I turned my face upward to see beautiful eyes of midnight blue.

"I never noticed how nice your eyes are Alex. Kiss me."

He stroked my hair. "No Maddie. You've been drinking. I don't think you're quite yourself. I want to kiss you, Maddie, but I want you to be sober. And to mean it."

"I mean it, Alex," I mumbled into his chest. "You're the best."

"I wish I believed that you believe that," said Alex with a sad smile. He disentangled my arms from his own and helped me to stand.

"Come on, Maddie. We're going to walk it off. I'll take you back to your cabin."

"No, Alex. I'm too tired. I'm going to crash right here, okay?" I climbed onto the bales of hay and hopped into the hayloft. I embraced the hay and fell right to sleep.

In the morning, I had a horrible headache, and I felt a crushing weight of guilt and anxiety on my chest. What happened last night? How did I get here? More importantly, whose arm was around me?

I lifted my head and saw Alex lying beside me on the hay. I saw that he had put a clean blanket over us both. I looked at his face, peaceful in sleep. He looked like an angelic little boy. My heart melted in my chest. I pulled the blanket up to his chin and stood up, careful not to make a sound. Maybe I could slip away and avoid embarrassment? No such luck.

"Hey," said Alex, his voice full of sleep. "You don't get to spend the night and slip away in the morning! What kind of lover are you, anyway?"

"The virtuous kind," I laughed. I sat back down beside him, feeling awkward.

"Alex, I'm so sorry about last night."

He studied me. "It's okay; you were scared. I'm just glad Manning didn't hurt you."

I sighed heavily. I wasn't sure that was true. Clayton made me crazy, shattered my heart. Rendered me powerless against my better judgement.

"Well, I hope I didn't do anything to hurt you, Alex," I said, looking at him lying there. "I get like this, sometimes. A bit ... manic. I don't know if Cassie told you about my illness."

Alex sat up on one elbow and gazed at me. "Not really. She said you were stressed—overworked."

I looked away, watching dust-motes float through a golden sunbeam that poked through the wooden slats of the wall.

"That's only part of it: I have a mood disorder," I said, hugging my knees. "Bipolar, probably. My doctor is still trying to sort it out. I feel things more deeply than most people, I think." I paused, trying to keep the nerves out of my voice. I hadn't really shared this information with anyone apart from my Mom.

"My emotions get too large... they take over. I'm either soaring high and nothing can touch me, or I'm so low down I feel like I will never see happiness again. And I have rapid cycling between the two states. I'm taking a medication that's helping, but... I still have to be careful." I exhaled, my shoulders dropping.

Alex came and sat down beside me. Then I felt his strong arms around me. "You never did do anything half-way, did you, Maddie?" I smiled, my head grazing his shoulder. I knew I could confide in Alex. I knew he wouldn't think I was crazy.

"Nope. You got that right. I'm sorry I got carried away last night.... I wasn't myself."

"It's no big deal, Maddie. You were very sweet."

"Was I?" My breath caught in my chest. A foggy memory of the night before started to come back to me.

"Alex, I ...."

"No, you don't have to say it. It's okay. I know you didn't mean those things you said. I'm your friend, and I always will be."

"You're wonderful, Alex," I said, taking a deep breath. "Maybe we could be something more to each other someday."

Alex was silent. Too silent. I dared to look at him briefly. He was staring off into space, and I couldn't read his face. He broke away, then stood up, reaching down to pull me up to his level. Then he looked into my eyes, and I saw an unexpected pain.

"Don't give me false hope, Maddie," he said finally. "I know you still have feelings for Manning. I won't be the second choice, okay?"

I held my breath. He was right. I did still have Clayton in my system, like a poison, like an addiction. And I hated myself for it.

Alex turned and jumped down from the loft to the bales of hay below. "Come on," he said looking up, his brows furrowed and jaw set tight. "Let's concentrate on finding proof of John's killer. Then maybe we can move on with our lives."

I jumped down with less enthusiasm. I was conflicted, confused: emotionally I felt raw, like an open sore. To top it all off, all my muscles seemed stiff and heavy this morning.

"Alex?"

"Yeah, Maddie?"

"Thanks for listening." Alex's mouth slid into a smile and the sun came out again in my world.

"Anytime, Maddie."

"I'm glad you're going to help me find Uncle John's killer, Alex. I don't want to do this alone… Where do we start?" I stretched my arms over my head, willing my energy to return.

"I think we've got to rule out our suspects one by one. You talk to Alvira about her mother, and I'll talk to George."

I nodded, stifling a yawn. "Okay. We can meet back here later, maybe, before dinner time."

I hesitated a moment before leaving the barn. Alex was so good to me, and I had behaved so badly. In a burst of affection, I gave him a brief squeeze. Then before he could say anything, I walked quickly away.

CHAPTER TWENTY-FOUR

Wren's Bakery and Grill was bursting with locals that morning. I sat down at a table, my stomach telling me I needed food, and fast. I was hoping Alvira would be the one to serve me, but it was another girl, Vicky. She was blonde and round and had a permanent smile on her face.

"What can I get for ya, hon?" She said, in a slow, rural drawl.

"I'll start with coffee, please. Is Alvira working today?"

"Nope, it's her day off. I think she might be at the town hall practicing for the play. She a friend of yours?"

"Yes, well, we met at my Aunt's."

I ordered eggs and bacon with home fries and looked around at the other guests. It surprised me to see Tuppence and Thalia talking and laughing at one of the other tables. That was interesting, I thought. I didn't know they were friends. But then, why not? I figured they knew each other through Cassie. They were both there the night John died.

I remembered the oleander bushes outside of Thalia's B&B. If she were friends with Thalia, it would have been easy for Tuppence to get the oleander ahead of time and take some of its leaves. It would be much easier to access Thalia's bushes with no one noticing. The bushes in the back garden of Green Briar were in plain sight. Thalia's bushes were not so obvious.

The food was delicious. I gobbled it up then paid my bill. Before I left, though, I walked up to Thalia and Tuppence's table.

"Hello strangers," I said smiling. "Enjoying your breakfast?"

"Oh, Maddie, honey! Come sit with us!" said Thalia with a gracious gesture.

"Well, I've already finished breakfast, but I can sit with you for a minute." I sat beside Tuppence because Thalia, being a big woman, filled the entire bench with herself.

"How are you doing, Maddie? How is Cassie?" asked Thalia with concern.

"As well as anyone can hope. Thanks for asking," I said. "It's been a tough few weeks." Thalia nodded in understanding.

I turned to Tuppence. "Do you know if Alvira's at the Playhouse today? I wanted to visit her."

Tuppence nodded. She was wearing dangle earrings, and they jingled when she moved.

"Yes, I think so. They have practice until noon. If you want to catch her, you'd better hurry."

Tuppence smiled sweetly at me, her eyes hidden behind her dark lashes, but I noticed she twisted the edge of her silk scarf rather violently under the table as she talked. Was she upset about the conversation we had with Cassie the other day?

I nodded and said my good-byes. I wondered what Tuppence thought about my visit with Alvira. I shivered a little, feeling her eyes follow me as I left the building. I parked my Nissan in the municipal parking lot across from the theatre. It started to snow, lacy white flakes floating across the sky. They landed on my hair and nose and made me sneeze.

"Bless you," said a familiar voice. It was the lady from the corner store, Mrs. Tilly. I knew her husband also ran the used bookstore and tea shop.

"Are you going to the theatre, too?" she asked. I nodded, smiling. She looked different without her shop apron, and her red hair was loose, instead of up in a bun. She looked at me down her beaky nose, her eyebrows arched in question.

"Oh Maddie, are you trying out for the play?" Mrs. Tilly asked, full of excitement. "I'm hoping to get the part of Mrs. Cratchit. There aren't a lot of women in A Christmas Carol, and Mrs. Cratchit is the perfect part for me, anyway. She's feisty like me and makes the most of her poverty. She knows how to stretch a meal and wears second-hand clothes." Her eyes were shining. Mrs. Tilley was already getting into character.

"Oh, they're doing A Christmas Carol. No, Mrs. Tilly, I'm not trying out. I'm just here to see a friend: Alvira Minton."

"Ah, yes. The naughty elf," said Mrs. Tilly with a wry expression. "She's a real individual, that one. Made her character a few years ago and has played the same role ever since." She shook her head. "I shouldn't wonder that she hates to perform the same role over again, but I know the children love it. They expect it every year now."

I nodded. "Yes, that's what she told me. I think she's gonna do a different take on the Christmas elf this year, though."

"Oh, I'd like to see that."

We had crossed the street and had arrived at the big double doors to the Playhouse.

We walked in, and it took a few moments for my eyes to adjust to the dark of the theatre.

"You know, this used to be a courthouse," said Mrs. Tilly. "They used to have sessions where the stage is now. There have even been rumours of ghosts haunting it over the years."

Mrs. Tilly clapped her hands together. "Oh, I knew it! See there on Centre Stage? Mr. Bryant, the school principal, is trying out for the Narrator. He'll be a shoo-in."

A deep rich voice echoed from the stage:

Scrooge looked about him for the Ghost and saw it not. As the last stroke ceased to vibrate, he remembered the prediction of old Jacob Marley, and lifting up his eyes, beheld a solemn Phantom, draped and hooded, coming, like a mist along the ground, towards him.

A shiver went down my spine. A larger than life robed figure, glowing, appeared on the stage.

"Wow, you were right: He has a great stage voice!" I exclaimed.

"Yes, Mr. Bryant is a wonderful speaker," said Mrs. Tilly. "Oh, look! I think I see Alvira peeking out from behind the curtain now!"

I thanked Mrs. Tilly and hurried down the right aisle towards the stage. Steps were leading to a doorway in the left wing of the stage. I walked upstairs and saw Alvira looking onto Stage Left from behind the curtains.

"Alvira!" I whispered as loud as I could. She turned and looked at me, shaking her head. She was in full costume as one of Santa's elves, a green shirt, black belt and green skirt and tights. I saw that her long hair was tucked in to a pointed elf's cap. Her eyes, mascaraed black and tilted, made her look different, sinister even—except for the bright smile she had for me.

"Maddie, so glad you came! I'm going run through my bit for the intermission. Then I can visit with you, okay?"

I nodded, spellbound. I hadn't been backstage since third grade, and I was enjoying this.

The scene with the ghost ended, and Alvira jumped out onstage with catlike grace. She laughed with theatrical mirth and danced, twirling around and jumping with high kicks into the air. Then she turned and faced the empty chairs in the audience.

"Ho, you boys and girls on Santa's naughty list, Take Warning! I am a naughty elf who will visit you on Christmas night with frightful tricks! The Ghost of Christmas Past is a pussycat compared to me!" Alvira's eyes flashed. She pulled down the painted cardboard scenery then stomped on it, laughing wildly. She raised her arms out as if to put a spell on the crowd. Then, she left to the wings of Stage Right.

Every actor and stagehand in the theatre was silent, stunned. Then the lights came on, and a voice came over the loudspeaker.

"Alvira, what was that all about? Come back to Centre Stage at once!" I heard a giggle from behind me. She must have gone back to the dressing rooms and around.

"Maddie, I'll meet you out in the parking lot," Alvira whispered, still giggling. She pulled off her elf's cap and ran a hand through her long brown hair, now cascading down around her shoulders. She grabbed up a coat from a coatrack beside the stairs and disappeared backstage. I shook my head.

Pretty gutsy, I thought. Full points for originality. I bet the kids loved her slapstick antics. I stepped down the stairs and headed back up the aisle to the main doors. I could hear murmuring, as people were still milling about, looking for Alvira. I slipped outside.

I waited across the street until I saw a girl in a large cape with a hood approach.

"Alvira?"

"Yep, it's me. Do you want to get a coffee at the bookstore cafe? We can walk there from here."

"Yeah, okay. Sounds good."

I left my car and headed off down the street with Alvira. She looked at me coyly.

"So, what did you think of my character?

"Well, she was certainly very original and unexpected. I'm not sure the director was so thrilled with it, though."

Alvira laughed bitterly. "Bill isn't happy with anything I do. I don't know why he wants me in the play. I wish he would just fire me."

"He can't fire you. You're all volunteers."

"Yeah, well, if he told me to quit, I would do it in a minute."

"But Alvira, if you hate it that much, why don't you quit yourself?"

She sighed. "You don't understand, Maddie, what it's like being the daughter of my mother. You just don't say no to her."

We had reached the door of the Kenowa Bookstore and Tea Shoppe. My eyes travelled the sign painted in an old-fashioned script to the books and antique teacups artfully arranged in the window. I felt right at home. Books were my first love, and I've already said how books and tea go together. I had already been here twice to replenish my growing stockpile and had decided this was far and away my favorite place in town.

We entered the building, and the doorbell signaled our presence. Mr. Tilly smiled at us from the counter.

"What will it be today, ladies?" he asked.

"Well, I'll have a peppermint mocha," I said, looking at the choice of drinks on the board.

"Me too," said Alvira nodding. "And a double-chocolate brownie."

We paid for our treats and put them down at a table for two. Books and literary curios lined the walls. I looked at them longingly. I knew I would be browsing for a book after our chat.

"So, tell me about the theatre," I said, breathing in the delicious peppermint chocolate aroma. "Have you taken dance? You look so at home on the stage."

Alvira glowed. "Thanks. I guess it's a gift. I do enjoy it

somewhat; I just would rather get some different roles once in a while. And yes, I have taken dance. Mother put me in dance when I was very young."

"So talented… and into science, too!"

Alvira laughed. "Yes. I know that might be hard to believe. It's a little unusual for an artsy type."

"I don't know about that. Why can't people be interested in diverse subjects? Look at Alex, he's into farming and also loves poetry and geology. I'm a nurse, and I like to write poetry. I think people have got to get away from old stereotypes, you know? We don't all fit into a pat little box."

Alvira stared at me, her face shining. "You're so right, Maddie! I knew you'd be different from the other girls in this town! I just knew we'd get along!"

I smiled, feeling a little shy.

"Alvira, tell me about yourself. What do you do for fun? Do you have a boyfriend?"

"Well, there isn't anything much to do for fun round here except maybe the dance hall. I used to dance all the time, back when I had a steady boyfriend. Since he's out of the picture, I don't go there anymore."

"What happened?"

Alvira shrugged. "I don't like to talk about it much. Besides, I'm over it."

Poor kid. Not lucky in love, either. I steered the conversation back to her mother.

"So, what do you think of your mother's art?" I asked, taking another sip of my coffee.

"Oh, she's brilliant, I guess. Everyone says so," said Alvira looking suddenly bored. I leaned forward.

"The other day, when we saw you in the gallery, Alex and I saw a painting she was working on. It was a portrait of John."

Alvira nodded, biting her lip.

"There was a photo on the canvas," I continued, "That showed your mother with her arm around John, and, well, Alex and I thought—"

"You thought they might have been an item back then, right?" said Alvira, her hands cradling her pixie face.

"Well, you're right, they were. They were very close. They were engaged to be married. Then Cassie came and swept John away from under her feet," Alvira said, sounding matter-of-fact.

"I'm glad Cassie did, because Mom would never have met my Dad and I wouldn't be here."

"That's understandable," I smiled. "But do you think she forgave him for leaving her? How did they stay friends all these years?"

Alvira looked troubled. "Well, I think she tried to forgive them. I thought she did—but I wondered when I saw the paintings."

"Paintings? Of John? She did more than one?" I asked, my heart skipping a beat.

"Yes," said Alvira shrugging. "She kept them hidden, out of sight. But she has done at least ten different paintings of John over the years. At least."

I couldn't believe what I was hearing. "Didn't you think that was a bit obsessive?"

Alvira looked at me cooly, shrugging her shoulders. "It's obsessive. But that's my mother. She obsesses about beautiful things. And she has trouble taking no for an answer. That's why I'm still in this awful play."

I pondered this confirmation in silence. Tuppence Millard had carried a flame for John. And she didn't take no for an answer. Had she killed him in a fit of rage, when he did not return her affections? The paintings weren't substantial proof of anything, but things were not looking good for Tuppence.

"Well, I'm gonna to look around for a book, now," I said finishing my coffee and rising to my feet. "I've got to get back before dinner."

"Oh, okay."

Alvira looked suddenly desolate, and I felt bad. It must be hard to grow up in your mother's shadow and have no real social life of your own. Then I had an idea.

"Why don't you join us for dinner? Aunt Cassie always makes enough to feed an army; it wouldn't be a problem."

Alvira brightened. "Oh, do you think so?"

"Yes, I do. I'll just call her on my cell to make sure it's okay. Then we can pick out some books together."

CHAPTER TWENTY-FIVE

Cassie had no problems with an extra dinner guest. She had made a roast of lamb with mint sauce and gravy, and it filled the place with delicious smells.

I was bursting to tell Alex what I had found out about Tuppence's paintings of John, but that would have to wait until after Alvira left. Alvira was chatting it up with Randy and Alex. I was glad she was enjoying herself.

I noticed that Alvira seemed to want to monopolize Alex's attention. It annoyed me to feel a little prick of jealousy. That was just silly: I had no claim on Alex. He was free to talk to anyone he wanted.

At that moment there came a knock at the door. Aunt Cassie, ran to answer it, her eyes bright.

"This way, Dr. Manning. It's so good of you to come."

My heart raced. No. It couldn't be.

"I've made a nice lamb for us tonight. You can sit here beside Maddie."

Oh yes, it was.

I could feel Clayton's eyes boring into me.

"I didn't know you'd be joining us, Dr. Manning," I said stiffly.

Clayton smiled. "I didn't know it either, until this afternoon.

I met your Aunt in town, and she was complaining about her arthritis. I gave her a prescription for something that could help, and she invited me here this evening. How could I refuse?"

How indeed? I bristled.

"What did you do today, Alex? Did anything exciting happen while I was away?" I asked, not daring to look over at Clayton. I felt my face growing hot.

"Well, other than the regular farm chores, I had a visit from George," said Alex, meeting my eyes.

"Did you tell him about the Hunt Club?" asked Aunt Cassie passing Alvira the potatoes.

"What's this about the Hunt Club?" asked Alvira.

"Well, George wants to hunt at Green Briar again. These were the original Algonquin hunting grounds of his people, you know. I've decided he can go ahead with it." Cassie's eyes looked a little moist. I supposed she was still struggling with her decision.

Alvira groaned. "Not the Hunt Club again. That means my Mom will probably want to join. I don't know why a woman who loves painting wildlife would want to hunt animals, do you?"

"Remember our conversation earlier today?" I asked, smiling. "People can have different interests. We don't all fit into tight stereotypes."

"Okay, I know, but I still hate it. It seems barbaric to me," Alvira looked green at the thought of it. I could sympathize. I felt a little that way at first, too. I realized that it was just part of living off the land here in the country.

"When are you going hunting?" asked Alvira. She wasn't looking very healthy. I was starting to worry.

"George wants to go tomorrow. I have a lot of work to do, but he's keen, so I guess I'll go with him. I think Randy and Spooky Joe; two George's friends and your Mom might come along."

"Would it be okay if I joined you, too?" asked Clayton smiling. I looked at Clayton in surprise. Alex glared at the floor. "Yeah, I guess so," Alex muttered ungraciously.

"You could stay the night Dr. Manning, and I could lend you one of John's hunting jackets," said Cassie.

"Then it's settled," said Clayton smiling. "I haven't been hunting in years, you know. I think I'm going to enjoy this."

I almost choked on a mouthful of mashed potato. It was clear I was not immune to stereotypes, myself: I would not have guessed in a million years that Clayton was interested in hunting. He didn't seem the type at all. Impeccably dressed, I figured he was too civilized for gritty country stuff.

"I didn't know you hunted," I said, looking at him with narrowed eyes.

"I'm sure there's a lot you don't know about me, Maddie," Clayton said, looking at me, meaningfully.

Just then Alvira stood up, swaying a little.

"Are you okay, dear? You're not looking very well at all."

"I—I think I just need to lie down for a minute."

"Of course. I'll get a bed ready for you. It's getting dark, and that snow is coming down hard. Maybe you should stay the night. I'll call your mother. It's a good job we have a doctor in the house."

Alvira allowed Clayton and Alex to lead her to one of the back bedrooms where she laid down and curled up in the blankets.

"Is she okay?" Aunt Cassie asked Clayton as he came out of the bedroom.

"She'll be fine. No fever, just a little light-headed. She's probably just fighting something. I'll keep an eye on her over the night."

Alex told Clayton to be up at dawn, to be ready for the hunt. Then he left to go out to the barn. I slipped out unannounced behind him.

"Alex, wait!" I called after him.

"What is it, Maddie?" he asked, not looking at me.

"I'm sorry I didn't see you before dinner, I had Alvira with me."

"Yeah, okay," he said, his voice lifeless.

"I wanted to tell you about something Alvira told me."

"Okay, what is it?" said Alex, not breaking his stride. I hurried to keep up.

"She said Tuppence had lots of paintings of John, not just the one we saw—which just proves she obsessed over him. We were right about their relationship, too—they were about to get married when Cassie came in and stole him away."

Alex stopped and looked at me, no expression on his face.

"That's pretty incriminating, don't you think?" I urged.

Alex frowned. "Well, it gives her a motive. But we still don't have proof." He turned to go.

"Alex!" I called after him.

"Yes?" he asked, his back still to me.

"If Tuppence is the killer, do you think Aunt Cassie's in any danger?"

"I don't know, Maddie," he said.

"Alex, I'm worried something will happen."

He turned to me then, his eyes blazing. "Why don't you go to your smooth-talking doctor for comfort, then?" He said this quietly, but his voice quivered with emotion. "I can't stop you."

"Alex, that's not fair!" I stormed. "I didn't invite him here. Aunt Cassie did. And he's still a suspect!"

"Yeah, well, I saw the way you two looked at each other at dinner, Maddie. There's no denying there's something there." Alex looked at me with such hurt and disdain that my chest tightened, and I found it hard to breathe.

"Alex ...." My eyes pleaded with him, but he had turned to stone.

"You don't deny it, do you? Right. Because it's true. Well, if you are foolish enough to fall for a slippery eel like Clayton Manning, that's your prerogative. There's nothing I can do to save you. See you later, Maddie."

Alex turned and walked into the barn. I stood in the snow feeling like I had just had my insides burned out.

I went back into the house to get my books, still feeling an ache in my heart. What Alex had said to me still stung. I didn't want to probe that wound too deeply. I might not like what I saw.

I heard Aunt Cassie's voice coming from the Great Room, and I went to say goodnight, books in hand.

"Oh, Maddie," she said when she saw me. "Come join us for tea, dear."

My heart sank even lower. Clayton—the last person I wanted to see—was sitting in the wing-backed chair by the fire, leaning over the arm, his face cupped in his hand. His shirt and hair were a little disheveled, but somehow, he maintained a look of refinement that was so much a part of him. He turned his bright eyes on me.

"Hi, Maddie. What are you reading?" He nodded to the pile of books in my arms.

I sat down in the chair opposite Aunt Cassie, feeling trapped. I wanted to run in the other direction, but I couldn't do that to my Aunt. I knew she thought she was doing me a favor inviting Clayton like this. She loved match-making, especially when it concerned me. She couldn't have guessed anything about the conflict going on inside me.

"I uh, haven't decided yet. I have a few mysteries to choose from. Some Agatha Christie, some Elizabeth Peters. Oh, and a book on Romantic Poetry—you know, Wordsworth and Coleridge. Also, some Hopkins." I set the books down on another chair beside me.

Clayton smiled. "And you're going to read all that tonight?"

"Not tonight—of course not. I'll pick one. Or two. I'll finish in a few days if I don't get too busy with other things."

"You always were such an avid reader," said Aunt Cassie picking up her sewing. "I remember when you came to stay with us as a girl, I had to raid the used book store for you constantly, to keep up."

"Ever heard of a library?" asked Clayton, eyebrows raised.

"In Kenowa? It's so small, Maddie was out of books in no time," Aunt Cassie smiled.

She turned to me. "Help yourself to some tea, dear. The tea service is here, but you can get another cup from the kitchen."

I got up with some relief and entered the kitchen, glad to be alone for a moment to catch my breath. But I wasn't alone for long. I took a cup from the cupboard and was rinsing it in the sink when Clayton came up behind me and slipped his arm around my waist.

"Can I help?" he asked, nuzzling my neck.

I startled, pulling away, but I felt my knees go weak.

"Don't—please."

"If I read your signals right, I think you like it. Tell me the truth, Maddie—Am I wrong?" He put a hand under my chin so I would have to look up at him. His eyes challenged me. I swallowed. Then I dodged him, taking my cup into the living room.

Aunt Cassie must have guessed something was up. She excused herself and headed off to bed.

"I'll leave the clearing up to you two," she said pleasantly. "Dr. Manning, don't forget to check in on Alvira. Your room is the one next to hers, beside the bathroom. And can you put out the fire for me? I'll see you and Maddie in the morning." She bent and kissed my forehead. Dear sweet Aunt Cassie, I thought. If you only knew the danger you could put me into… Unfortunately, she couldn't read my mind. She disappeared down the hallway to her bedroom, leaving me alone with the one person I had been so desperately trying to avoid.

"I should go, too," I said nervously, starting to pick up my books off the chair but ending up knocking the pile to the floor.

"At least stay and finish your tea, Maddie," said Clayton helping me scoop the books up onto a side table.

I hesitated, then sat down opposite Clayton. "Okay. One cup of tea. Then I have to go."

Clayton shrugged, smiling. Then he turned serious.

"Maddie, can I ask you something?"

"Okay," I said, looking into the fire. I held my breath.

"What are you afraid of?"

I nearly spilled my tea into my lap. "Pardon?"

He smiled. "You know what I think, Maddie? I think you're afraid of letting go. Of feeling too much. Your emotions have betrayed you in the past, and you are trying hard not to give into them. Am I right?"

I sucked in a breath. Wow, I thought. A direct hit. "Maybe I'm just careful about making decisions," I said slowly. "I don't like to make mistakes."

"You mean, there's someone else?" His eyes probed me intelligently. You are much too clever, Dr. Manning, I thought to myself.

"Maybe. I don't know."

"We could settle this the old-fashioned way. I could challenge him to a duel." Clayton made a wry face, and I laughed in spite of myself.

"There you are!" he said. "There's the Maddie I've been missing! It's good to see you smile."

I looked away, into the fire. "I'm sorry, Clayton. I don't mean to be so prickly. You're right. I don't want to give in to my emotions. Once I can trust someone completely, though, I can let go."

"So why don't you trust me? Is it the medical inquiry? Or my breakdown afterwards?" Clayton regarded me with a curious expression. I squirmed in my seat.

"No. I think what you went through was understandable. It's hard for doctors to get through their careers without someone accusing them of doing a bad job."

Clayton nodded. "That's the sad truth of it. So, what is it, Maddie? What can I do to earn your trust?"

I took a breath in. "Well, I guess, for starters you could tell me about your research. You know, the research you gave your talk about in Vancouver. Wasn't it on oleander?" I watched for his reaction.

Clayton started in surprise. He wasn't expecting this.

"What? No! Well, I guess, in a way. It's a replication of a constituent of oleander, made in a lab. We have been giving it to cancer patients in hospital trials."

He shook his head and gave a low whistle of comprehension.

"So that's it. I don't believe it! You think I gave John the oleander in his tea? Maddie, don't be ridiculous!"

"Alex told me that John had leukemia. I thought maybe you had given him the drug to see if you could fight it you know and maybe used too much." It sounded weak to my ears now. I was beginning to think—hope—I had been wrong.

"You think very little of my medical skills, I see. And my judgement." He thought about this for a moment.

"What else has Alex been saying about me, Maddie?" said Clayton, his jaw clenched tight. "Is he the one you're conflicted about? I don't care much for the competition: He seems pretty desperate if he has to poison your mind against me."

I felt my face growing hot.

"I think I should leave now," I said quietly, gathering my books and heading for the door. "Good night, Clayton."

He was silent, looking into the fire as I gathered my books and left. I took off into the woods, my face wet with tears.

CHAPTER TWENTY-SIX

My dreamcatcher was not working very well; nightmares plagued my sleep. My dreams were full of sharp claws and teeth, belonging to shadowy monsters ready to rip me open and spill my red insides out onto the snow. They were the hunters, and I, their prey. My blood was pumping fast, a loud drumbeat hammering in my ears. I awoke in a sweat.

It was just six o'clock in the morning, and I sat up in bed, wide awake. I heard voices outside. Who else was up at this hour? Then I heard a single gunshot and remembered. The Hunt Club. This was the day they were starting the hunt.

Hope was sleeping at my feet, and I had to move her gently to get up. Of course, she woke up anyway and followed me into the kitchen. I looked at her with affection. My little friend, I thought. At least you won't leave me.

I drew open the cottage curtains and looked out the window at the still-night sky. It was only just beginning to lighten. I hadn't thought about how close the hunt would be to my cottage. I wondered if it was safe to go up to the house in a few hours, for breakfast. Feeling a little anxious, I made myself a bracing cup of tea and sat down on the couch.

I grabbed up one of the books I had bought the day before

and started to read. It was a beautiful book of poetry by Gerard Manley Hopkins. I had read it many times before, but his poetry helped calm me when I was on edge like this. I opened the book and read an excerpt from the poem "Peace":

When will you ever,
Peace, wild wood-dove,
shy wings shut,
Your round me roaming end,
and under be my boughs?

I closed my eyes. Maybe I would find that peace of soul that Hopkins sought. Not today, though. Not all bound up with emotion like this. I thought about what Clayton had said to me last night. Clever Clayton. He had cut through all my defenses. I was terrified of letting go, of being ruled by my emotions. Afraid of losing control. Why? Because I had lost control before. I felt things much too deeply. And my past was never far away.

I reached over and grabbed a couple of orange pills from the bottle I had left on the coffee table. These were helping to keep my moods more stable, but they weren't the only thing I had to rely on. I had to be stronger. I had to be me. Then maybe I could figure out my own heart.

I gazed out the window, remembering a line of poetry by Tagore that Alex had recited the other day: "When the voice of the Silent touches my words, I know him and therefore know myself." I breathed in and out, meditating on words I knew to be true.

Then I picked up my journal and pen and began to write, the ink flowing out onto the page like a balm to my soul. My mind stretched out to the forest, to the silent snow, and I wrote:

Shelter me, gentle forest
Spirit, wreathed
In robes of white
Wrap me round
Within thy womb
Keep circling wolves away

Outside your pine walls
Death, unspeakable
Crushing of teeth
Crunching of bones
Terror incarnates
Blood of kin and fey

I stared at the lines I had written, horrified. Where had that come from? The hunt was infecting me, getting under my skin, when I had hoped to find myself on the page. I snapped the book shut, startling the cat who moved off the couch in search of a less dangerous place to sleep.

On edge, I went to make myself another tea. The first one had not helped my nerves. I walked over to the kitchen I glanced out of the cottage window and heard three sudden shots in rapid succession. My hand jerked, and I dropped my teacup, shattering it on the floor.

"Sorry, Hope. It's okay," I said to the poor cat who was now cowering in the corner. I don't think I sounded convincing, though, because she took off into the bedroom with a strangled mew. I took a deep breath to slow down my heartbeat. Then I went in search of a broom and dustpan.

I had just cleaned up the mess I had made when there was a frantic knock at the door.

I opened it to find Alex, wide-eyed and panting.

"Alex, what is it?" I cried. The anxiety gripping my chest grew stronger. I knew something would happen, and finally, it was here, staring me in the face.

"Maddie," he said, out of breath, "There's been a horrible accident. I think George is dead."

"George Riddleman?" I grabbed my shoes. That was not what I had expected. "Has anyone called an ambulance?"

"Yes," he said, looking stricken. "I don't know what else to do. He was bleeding out everywhere. Oh, God help me," He screened his face with his fingers. "I think it was me."

"It's okay, Alex. Don't worry about that right now. Everything's going to be okay." Inside, I wondered if that were true.

"Is Clay—Dr. Manning on the scene?" I asked.

Alex nodded. I relaxed just a little. "Well, let me go and help him. Though, I don't think there's much more we can do."

I opened the door, ready to go, when I paused for a moment, looking at Alex's pale face. His jaw was set, his broad shoulders were tensed, ready to fight. But in his eyes, I saw a little boy needing comfort. I took his hand and squeezed it.

"Come on. Lead the way." Alex seemed to grow stronger from my touch. He flashed me a grateful smile and hurried forward.

We wound through the forest, branches slashing at our faces and hands. The newly fallen snow pulled at our boots, slowing our progress. Just when I despaired at ever getting there, we saw the ambulance attendants carrying a shrouded body on a stretcher. I stopped in my tracks, knowing there was nothing more to be done.

"Show me where you found him," I said to Alex, my breath sending a frozen spray into the air.

"Over there," Alex pointed to a tall evergreen and behind which I could just make out the bloodstains in the snow. I turned to talk to Alex, but two police officers beckoned him away. I looked around for a familiar face. There were other police officers and first-responders, some of them talking to an old man with a beard, a couple of young fellows I didn't know, Randy and Tuppence Millard.

Then I spotted Clayton, looking grim. He nodded to me as I came near.

"Is he dead?" I asked.

"Yes," he said simply. "There was nothing I could do. The bullet had already done its damage."

"Alex thinks it was him. An accident," I said in a low voice. I glanced back at Alex, who was leaning against the great pine tree, looking stunned. He was being questioned by two officers, while Detective Inspector Rebecca Trent took careful notes and scanned the site of the death.

Clayton shook his head. "It was no accident, Maddie. Whoever shot George did it point blank, up close."

"How do you know?" I asked.

"The bullet wound was straight through the heart, and there was an abrasion ring, something only seen when the muzzle of a gun has touched the body. George didn't have a chance."

I stared at him in horror. It was a cold-blooded murder. Feeling dizzy, I reached for a tree-branch in my effort to keep grounded. I couldn't be certain about the first murder, but this time there was no mistaking it. There was a killer on the loose.

The branch I was holding snapped, and I struggled to regain my balance.

"Whoa there, Maddie. Are you okay?" Clayton asked, his voice filled with concern. He grabbed hold of my arm.

"I'm fine," I said. But I wasn't sure that was true. The lack of sleep and constant anxiety were wearing me down. There didn't seem to be an end to that now.

"I think you should go into the house with Cassie," he said. "I should stay here a while longer. The police will want to talk to all the hunters."

I nodded. "Okay, that's a good idea. Does Aunt Cassie know about George?"

Clayton shrugged. "I'm not sure. Probably. The police would have come to the house. Go and see."

I nodded and started out into the forest. I looked back at Clayton in time to see the beautiful Detective Inspector Rebecca Trent coming to question him. I paused for a moment to listen, but they were speaking too low, heads bent together. I took a steadying breath. No time for feelings.

I wound my way through the forest back to the well-worn path from the cottage. Thoughts raced through my mind as I sloshed through the snow. It made little sense. Who would have wanted to kill George? Tuppence was out on the hunt; she had the opportunity. But what was the motive? If something connected the two murders, I was missing the link. What could it be?

When I got to the house, Aunt Cassie was in hysterics.

"This is my fault! I should never have let that horrible Hunt Club start up again!" she wailed. "I knew it was a terrible idea! John must be so disappointed in me!" She started sobbing, and I tried to console her.

"Aunt Cassie—Look at the facts," I admonished. "It is not your fault. And it is not the Hunt Club's either. There's no doubt, this was murder." I told her what Clayton had told me.

"But, I don't understand," she simpered, her hands clutching her chest. "Who would want to kill George? He was such a kind man." Then her eyes widened.

"Does his family know?" Aunt Cassie lay back in her armchair, looking faint.

"I'm sure the police will tell them." I put another log on the fire and poked at it. Somehow it didn't take the chill out of my bones.

We were silent, thinking about the implications of a murder so close to us. I felt sad, remembering that the gentle giant who had given me the dreamcatcher was now dead. Who would want to kill George? Had he known something we didn't?

Then I asked: "Aunt Cassie, do you know what John and George were arguing about, the day John died?"

Aunt Cassie hedged a bit. "Oh, well, I don't know dear, I think it was something about Randy."

"About Randy?" I asked in surprise. "Alex thought it was about the Hunt Club since George was always bringing it up."

"Well no, I don't believe it was," said Cassie blinking. "I think it was about Randy. Randy used to hunt with George on Spooky Joe's land, and they got to know each other pretty well. I think George worried about Randy. He didn't understand that Randy had autism. He thought the boy was, well, wrong-headed, let's say."

"George didn't want to hunt with Randy anymore," said Alvira coming through the doorway. "I overheard him say so. Randy didn't seem to have the same empathy for animals he hunted that George did. Or people, for that matter."

"The whole thing tore John to pieces," said Cassie, looking tired and weak. "He loved Randy like a son."

I wondered if that was entirely true. After all, John left his farm to Alex, not Randy. I wondered what Randy thought of that? I thought a good father or father-figure shouldn't show favoritism like that. It bred jealousy. I wondered, too, if Randy knew that George had argued with John about him? I didn't like where this line of thought was taking me.

"Are you feeling better, Alvira?" I asked, changing the subject.

"Yep, all better. It was just indigestion or something. I slept it off."

"Have you seen your mother, Alvira?" asked Cassie.

"Uh-huh. I went out to find her as soon as I heard about George. She's pretty shaken up. After the police are through with her, she'll come up to the house."

"They should all come up to the house to warm up and have some tea. Maddie, would you be a dear and fix them some tea and sandwiches? I'm not feeling very well. I think I'll have a nap."

"Sure, Aunt Cassie. You just rest here. I'll bring your tea and sandwiches when you're ready."

"I can help, too," said Alvira, her eyes bright.

"Thanks," I said smiling. "Better get started."

"You know, the police will probably have to get statements from us, as well," said Alvira, arranging the platter of fresh-made buns and deli meats and cheeses.

Alvira looked like she was enjoying this. She probably couldn't wait to get back to Wren's and start sharing the gossip with her coworkers.

I made a wry face. "It'll be a shame to wake Aunt Cassie. She's been through enough already. Well, we'd better put out more food, then. The police can have some too if they're allowed."

"Oh, they're locals. They won't stand on ceremony."

I put the water in the kettle and plugged it in. "So, George didn't like Randy?"

Alvira shook her head. "Not from what I heard. My mother sometimes hunted with George and Randy and a couple of other local boys up on Spooky Joe's land. She said George was afraid of him."

"Why would he be afraid of Randy?" I asked, puzzled.

"I dunno. People are always afraid of what they don't

understand."

I thought about this as I poured the hot water for the tea. Randy never showed much emotion, but he didn't seem like a bad guy. I had always enjoyed his company. He sometimes went off on rants about whatever his particular interest was, so it was hard to have a two-way conversation with him. But he was always knowledgeable and entertaining. I couldn't imagine why George would have feared him.

"Here, Alvira, you finish this platter. I'll ask Aunt Cassie if we can pull out some of her frozen treats. It's good she always bakes so much extra, for when she has company."

I walked back into the Great Room where Aunt Cassie was dozing by the fire. I sat for a minute, trying to get the nerve up to wake her. Then I looked out the windows and saw a whole pile of people coming out of the back forest toward the house. Here comes the cavalry, I thought grimly.

CHAPTER TWENTY-SEVEN

The police didn't stay long. They took our statements and left with the promise that they would be back. Only the beautiful Detective Inspector Trent stayed for tea. I noticed that she sat next to Clayton in the Great Room and wondered if that was significant. Those two seemed to have a lot to talk about. Alex and Randy brought extra chairs in from the kitchen and sat around the coffee table with Tuppence Millard and me.

"Are we all suspects then, Inspector Trent?" I inquired with exaggerated politeness. She looked at me as though I were an irritating insect she would like to squash.

"We're not sure of anything at the moment, Ms. Malone. The medical report will confirm whether we think this is a suspicious death."

"So, are we free to leave?" asked Alvira. "I've got to get back home. I've got to work at Wren's at one."

"For now. We may need you later for questioning," Ms. Trent said, and Alvira got up to go.

"I'll just take these dishes into the kitchen for you. Thanks for an interesting time. See you later, Maddie, Cassie."

I cringed. Like a murder was an everyday occurrence, a bit of entertainment. Amazing. Alvira's social blunders were almost an art form. "Never mind that, Alvira. You've got to go. I'll do it," I said, picking up the tray with the cheese plate.

"Let me help you," said Alex, rising to his feet.

"Oh, no, that's okay," I said, feeling Clayton's eyes on me. Never you mind, I thought viciously. You have your lady detective to keep you company.

"It's no trouble," said Alex, grabbing the tea service.

"Well, I think I'll be going, too," said Tuppence. "Call me if you need anything, Cassie."

"I'm going as well. I'll see you folks later," said Rebecca. "If anyone thinks of anything or sees anything suspicious, call me right away. I'll leave you my card." She put a pile of cards on the coffee table for us to take. Then she turned to Clayton. "Walk me out?" she asked. He nodded. The two of them left, deep in discussion. I disappeared into the kitchen with my dishes.

Alex washed the dishes, and I dried.

"Turns out you were right to worry, Maddie. Only it wasn't Cassie in danger; it was George."

I glanced over at him. That lock of brown hair was over one eye, while the other eye was narrowed. The effect was adorable.

"But I don't understand why it was George, do you? I mean, if we can connect the two murders."

"They're connected. They have to be. That's too much of a coincidence."

"But what's the connection?"

"Tuppence was at the scene; she could easily commit both murders."

"Yes, but she only has a motive for one," I said, reaching up to put the dishes in the cupboard.

"That we know of," Alex pointed out. "Maybe George knew something about John's death. Maybe she had to kill him to keep it quiet."

I thought about this. "Yes, that's possible. George could have seen something on the night John died, but if that were so, why wouldn't he go to the police?"

Alex shrugged. "Who knows? Maybe he was secretly in love with her? Or maybe she didn't know what he knew until he started blackmailing her."

"Okay, that works, but this is all supposition. We need hard evidence."

"Right. And there are other suspects we need to rule out."

I nodded. "I didn't want to bring this up to you, but ... do you know why George argued with John before he died?"

Alex shook his head. "Alvira and Aunt Cassie say he was arguing about Randy. They say George was afraid of Randy; that he didn't trust his moral judgement." Alex's face turned stormy. "I know what you're thinking. Don't even go there, Maddie! People don't understand Randy. He wouldn't hurt a flea. He just doesn't know how to express his emotions, you know?"

"I know," I said, laying a hand on Alex's arm. "I'm just looking at all the angles, that's all."

"What about your Dr. Manning?" asked Alex, avoiding my eyes. I took my hand away.

"He's not my Dr. Manning," I exclaimed. "What about him?"

"Manning's got to be a suspect too, doesn't he? He was there for both murders."

"He doesn't have a motive," I said quietly.

"Yes, he does," said Alex, triumphant. "George was the one who made the malpractice complaint."

I froze. "Are you sure?"

"Yep. He told us all himself. Cassie tried to talk him out of it, but he made the complaint, anyway."

"What was the complaint?" I asked, fidgeting with the dishtowel.

"He was being prescribed something experimental that he didn't need, at a dose that was too high and causing complications."

"What were the complications?"

Alex shrugged. "Not sure. Something that was causing abdominal bleeding."

I frowned. "That doesn't sound good."

Alex turned to me and put his hands on my arms, gentle but firm. "No, it doesn't. I know you don't want to hear this, but I worry about you, Maddie. I know you like to stay at the cottage by yourself, but don't you think, with a murderer running around, it would be wise to move to the house? There's plenty of room here: you could take the spare bedroom."

I thought about this. "Maybe you're right. I do sometimes get a little afraid at night. But what about my cat?"

"Hope can stay in the barn, that's where she came from. Or, I can ask Cassie if she'd mind Hope coming in the house."

"Oh, that would be better," I breathed. "I would miss her."

"Either that or you can sleep in the barn again," said Alex, grinning.

I fake-punched his arm. "Don't get any ideas, Mister," I laughed.

"Oh, I have lots of ideas." Alex flashed a mischievous smile. I smiled back, meeting his eyes. For a moment, my heart was at peace.

"Okay, I'm going down to the cottage to get my stuff. Do you have a box I could carry Hope in? A cat-carrier maybe?"

"No cat-carrier. Maybe a box. Here, why don't I come with you and help you?"

"No, it's okay. I can manage. I can just stick a few books in my overnight bag and carry Hope in my duffel bag."

"You're sure?" His midnight eyes probed mine. I flushed.

"I'm sure. I'll see you back here later."

CHAPTER TWENTY-EIGHT

That night, at the ranch house, I settled into my new room. I allowed Hope to roam the house, but she nestled in beside me in my four-poster bed. I had a good book beside me on the bedside table, and I had stolen a cup of tea from the kitchen to bring down the hall to my guest bedroom. Just as I was getting into bed, there was a knock on the door.

"Come in!" I called.

The door opened, and Aunt Cassie poked her head in the room.

"Just wanted to see if you needed anything dear," she said. "You look pretty cozy there. My, that cat has adopted you, hasn't she?"

I smiled and gave Hopes ears a little scratch. "Yes," I said, "she's a little gift from Uncle John, I think."

Aunt Cassie smiled broadly. "Yes, I'm sure John would have wanted you to have her. Well, goodnight dear, and sweet dreams."

I settled back down to read, but my mind was whirling. I kept going over the events of the day, trying to piece together what had happened. I couldn't get the horror of the murder out of my head. I sat up and took a sip of my tea.

Out of the corner of my eye, I noticed a blue duffel bag sticking out of the closet. I stared at it curiously for a moment, then hopped out of bed and walked across the floor. I grabbed up the bag and placed it on my bed. Hope was not amused at my interruption of her sleep. She strutted away, tail in the air, and hopped off the bed. Then she disappeared underneath it.

"Okay, I don't blame you. It's probably quieter under there," I laughed. I zipped open the blue bag, wondering if I wasn't too nosy. That didn't stop me, though.

I knew the bag belonged to Alvira when I saw in it the distinctive red sweater she had worn the day before. That made sense. She had slept in this room only yesterday: She must have left the bag behind because she was in such a hurry to get to work.

I lifted the sweater and found a makeup bag at the bottom. Still curious, I zipped open the make-up bag and found a photo inside along with lipstick and mascara. I held the photo up to the light. It was a picture of a group of people decked out in hunting gear. I recognized Uncle John, and George, Alex and Randy, an old man that must have been Spooky Joe, two younger men (which one was Steve Braeman, I wondered?) and then Tuppence. Standing next to Tuppence was Alvira. I flipped the photo over. I saw "The Hunt Club," scrawled across the back of it in pen. I stared at the handwriting wondering why it was so familiar. Then I realized it was the same hand that had signed the paintings of Tuppence Millard. This photo must have belonged to Alvira's mother.

I frowned. Why was Alvira in a photo with the Hunt Club? I didn't know she could even hunt. I supposed it made sense that she would have learned, with her mother being a hunter. Still, she had seemed so much against the whole idea. Frowning, I put the photo back in the make-up case and zipped up the tote bag. I would stop by Alvira's place in the morning and return it to her, I decided.

Hope had come back and was rubbing against me. "Meow," she said. I yawned and stroked Hope's fur.

"You're right, Hope. It's been a long day. Time to get to bed."

I woke late the next morning to the smell of bacon, sausage, eggs and coffee. I got dressed in a hurry and walked down to the kitchen where I saw Alex and Randy helping themselves to sausage and bacon. Aunt Cassie was pouring them coffee. She smiled at me as I came in.

"Good morning, Maddie. Help yourself." I didn't need any coaxing. It was almost as if yesterday hadn't happened, I thought to myself. It was strange how we clung on to the routines of life in the midst of death. Life went on. We ate, we slept, we banded together against the encroaching darkness.

Alex met my eyes as we both reached for the sugar bowl.

"Sleep well?" he asked. I nodded.

"Alvira left a duffel bag behind in my room. I'll return it to her today when I go into town." Then I asked: "Has Alvira ever been hunting with you?"

Alex looked at me, surprised, and shook his head. "No, never. Why?" I hesitated, not wanting to admit I had been snooping, at least in front of Aunt Cassie.

"The police were here again earlier," said Randy, interrupting between mouthfuls of bacon. "They were asking questions about the Hunt Club."

"They wanted permission to search the guest cottage, too," said Alex with a grimace.

I felt the bacon lodge in my throat. "The guest cottage? Why?"

"John's old antique rifle is missing," explained Aunt Cassie. "They think it was probably the murder weapon. They are out searching the grounds for it now."

I thought about this while taking a sip of the tea that Aunt

Cassie had poured for me. I had no problems with the police searching the cottage, but it did somehow feel like they were violating my privacy. I knew it was silly. The cottage wasn't mine. Still, I didn't relish the idea of them rifling through the place.

Alex seemed to understand what I was thinking. He looked at me, his expression one of sympathy.

"I'm sure they will be careful not to mess anything up," he said. We ate the rest of our breakfast in a heavy silence.

Afterward, we sat out in the great room, huddled by the fire. Then the doorbell rang. Aunt Cassie and I looked at each other. Was it the police again, with more questions?

It turned out to be Thalia, who burst into the room bearing gifts: a ham casserole that Thalia had made and a box of Black Gold. "Everyone needs chocolate in a crisis," said Thalia, hugging me.

Aunt Cassie took the casserole to the kitchen while the rest of us sat around the fire eating the chocolates. I picked a dark chocolate hazelnut cluster. Alex took a coffee-flavored one. Our hands touched briefly, and I looked up, meeting his eyes. I considered how Alex and I had sat down together on the couch. It had felt very natural. Now, I was suddenly too aware of him. And of Aunt Cassie's eyes focused on me like a beacon.

"I think I'll refill this teapot," I said, getting up from the couch. Alex followed me, carrying the tray. We met Aunt Cassie and Thalia coming out of the kitchen.

"Wait until you try some of my casserole, hun. It has fried plantains in it, just like they have in Puerto Rico," said Thalia smiling.

"Yes, I'll look forward to it Thalia, thank you," I said smiling back. "I'm pretty full right now, but I'll enjoy some of that later."

Alex and I continued into the kitchen. I was glad to get the chance to talk to him alone. I told him about the photo I had seen in Alvira's duffel bag.

"Why was she in the picture with the Hunt Club, when she didn't hunt?" I asked curiously. "You were there; you must remember something about it."

Alex frowned. "Yeah, I remember. Alvira was hanging around the Hunt Club a lot at that time. I thought she might have been thinking about trying hunting like her Mom. I also remember her flirting a lot with Matt Kroger. I think she might have been going out with him."

"Okay, but that doesn't explain why she would keep a picture of the Hunt Club in her make-up bag."

Alex shrugged. "Maybe she still has a thing for Matt. Although I hear he's about to be married, worse luck for Alvira."

I changed the subject. "You were out on the hunt, yesterday. Did you see anything suspicious?"

Alex shook his head. "I was out there a little later than the rest. I couldn't find some of my hunting gear. I was missing my first aid kit, and it had a copy of my hunting license in it. I told the others to go ahead; I would meet up with them at the big oak, it's the tallest tree in the forest and a good place to start. I told them I'd text them when I was ready."

"And did you?"

"Yeah, I was only a half-hour late. It was half-past six when I got there, and only Randy and Spooky Joe came to see me. They didn't know where Tuppence or George was. We tried texting him and called him but didn't get a response."

"What about Clayton," I dared to ask, avoiding Alex's eyes.

"Dr. Manning came five minutes later with the two local guys, the brothers — Matt and Derrick."

"But not Tuppence," I said thoughtfully.

"No, not until much later."

"I heard voices and a gunshot when I woke up around six," I said. "Did anyone else say they took a shot?"

Alex shook his head. "Nope."

We looked at each other, knowing I must have heard the fatal shot.

"Did you tell the police this, yet?" asked Alex. I nodded. "Yes, I told one of the young officers yesterday. He wrote it all down. At least we know the time of the murder."

Just then the doorbell rang again. We heard Aunt Cassie talking to someone but couldn't listen to what she was saying. A minute later she poked her head into the kitchen.

"Maddie, the police want to talk to you," she said, looking pale.

"To me?" I asked, dumbfounded.

"They've found John's old rifle," Aunt Cassie explained. "It was in the guest cottage."

CHAPTER TWENTY-NINE

I repeated my story to Inspector Trent, feeling more than a little frustrated and annoyed. I felt frustrated because she kept asking me the same questions over again and annoyed; because Inspector Trent looked impeccable in a form-fitting blue suit and not a beautiful hair out of place, while I was a mess both emotionally and physically.

"I already told you," I said irritably, "I heard the shot and some voices at six o'clock while I was making myself a tea."

"Are you normally up that early?" asked Rebecca, her perfectly drawn mouth in a tight knot of suspicion.

"Yes—no, not all the time. I have a mood disorder, so sometimes I sleep too much and at other times very little or not at all."

Ms. Trent was busy writing this all down. I was a little worried about how she would take this information. There are many misconceptions around mood disorders and a real range in severity. Maybe she would assume I was criminally insane. She was certainly treating me that way.

"Did you leave your cabin at any time?"

"Yes, I already told this to the other officer," I said, gathering my wild hair into a ponytail at the back of my head. A few wisps managed to escape, and I blew them out of my face.

"I left when Alex Bateman came to tell me about George's death."

"What time was that?" asked Ms. Trent, pen poised.

"I would say it was around seven o'clock. I'm pretty sure I had been up for an hour."

"Did you see anyone when you left the cottage, besides Alex?"

I shook my head.

"Did you take an antique rifle out of this house at any time, Ms. Malone?"

"No, I did not."

"Were you familiar with the rifle?"

"I saw John take a rifle hunting with him, but I never looked at it closely, and I don't even know where he kept it in this house. I'm not interested in hunting, Detective, and I've never even held a gun. Nor do I want to."

Detective Inspector Rebecca Trent wrote all this down, then snapped her notebook closed and stood up to leave. Our interview was finished.

"Okay, that's all for now, Ms. Malone," she said coolly. "Though we may need to question you later."

She left me sitting by the fire in the Great Room. As soon as she was gone, Thalia came to sit by my side.

"How horrible for you, dear," Thalia wailed. "That woman is a cool cucumber, I'm telling you. She's a cold piece of work."

"She's just doing her job, Thalia," said Cassie, squeezing my hand. "Don't worry. She can't seriously suspect you of murder, Maddie. You hardly knew the man, and the evidence is all circumstantial. Obviously, the murderer planted the rifle in the guest cottage to throw suspicion on you."

"Yes, but why?" I asked.

Cassie shrugged. "The cottage was close by. An easy choice."

I sighed. "I guess you're right. It worries me, though."

"I don't doubt it, what with a murderer running around out here!" said Thalia with emotion. "I think you and Cassie should both come and stay at my place for a while until the police have this cleared up."

"Oh, that's very nice of you, Thalia. But you've got the Bed and Breakfast to run, I don't know about Aunt Cassie, but I don't want to be in the way."

"She does have a point, honey," said Aunt Cassie, her hands clasping and unclasping as she sat in her favorite chair by the fire.

"Maybe we should go away for a few days. I can't sleep at night worrying about things and missing John. Alex and Randy will be okay on their own for a while."

I looked at her with concern. I knew she must be feeling very anxious to consider leaving her beloved Green Briar, even for a short while.

I took a deep breath. "Okay, Aunt Cassie. If it makes you feel better, let's do it. I'll pack up my things, and then I'll tell Alex. Is he out at the barn?"

"Yes, I think he had some chores left to do."

"You can go on ahead without me Aunt Cassie. You can ride with Mom and Thalia. I have a few things to do in town, so I'll come later."

"Okay, honey. Don't be long, though. I'll feel better if you're safe with us and out of this place." She looked at it sadly.

"It used to be my place of peace and solitude. Now it seems cursed."

"Don't say that, Aunt Cassie. As soon as the police catch the murderer, it will be peaceful again."

When I told Alex about our move, he looked relieved. "I'm glad, Maddie. I want you well out of harm's way. No more sleuthing, okay? Let the police handle it. I don't want you to be the next target."

He surprised me then, by putting arms around me. gentle and firm, drawing me into a sweet embrace. For a moment I stayed there with my head against his chest, feeling his heart beating faster. I looked up at him, enjoying the curve of his neck, breathing his scent, my lips close to his: I thought he might kiss me then, but he pulled away.

I stepped away, feeling self-conscious and shaky. I felt something powerful between us that had not been there before, and I wasn't sure what to do about it. Whatever it was, it would have to wait.

I took a breath. "See you, Alex," I said, keeping my voice light. "Be careful, okay?"

"Sure. Maybe I'll drop by and see how you're doing later on."

"No worries. I should be there before dinner. I've got to get some things at the convenience store, and I want to drop that duffel bag into Alvira. I'm sure she's missing it."

I drove along the winding country lane, thinking strange thoughts. I had thought I was in love with Clayton, but now I wasn't so sure. It flattered me that the suave, handsome doctor was interested in me, and part of what attracted me to him was his confidence, his sense of certainty. He had a dominant nature, used to exerting control. I felt like he could steer me in any direction, while I was floating directionless. I had to wonder if that was healthy.

When I was with Alex, I felt more at home. I liked the way he thought about things, his sensitive poet's soul and his love of the land. I liked that he loved animals and was not afraid to get his hands dirty. I enjoyed spending time with him. We had always been friends. But was that friendship with Alex deepening into something more?

I slowed my Nissan to a stop and turned left down Silver Mine Road, another winding country road that seemed to stretch on forever. I'd never been down here before; Aunt Cassie told me that Alvira lived in the big house at the end of the road with her mother. I glanced over at the duffel bag on the passenger's seat and wondered again about the Hunt Club photo. I wanted to ask Alvira about it, but she might not appreciate my going through her things.

The road was pretty but desolate. Except for an old farmhouse and a run-down shack, there was nobody there for miles. Even though I loved forests, I felt a little creeped out about the isolation. How could Alvira live down here? I felt sorrier for her than ever. Living in her mother's shadow and isolated from her age group like this, was it any wonder that she was a little odd and sought attention the way she did? She needed to get out on her own.

I thought about Alvira's mother, Tuppence Millard. Could she have been the one who planted the gun in the guest cottage? She had had the opportunity. Alex said she was the last to show up to the group looking for George. She could have shot George point blank around six o'clock that morning, circled back around through the thick forest and waited in the bush behind the cottage until she saw me leave with Alex out the front door. Then she could have planted the gun and gone to join the others. I would have to ask Alex if he noticed what direction she came from when she joined the group. But if so, what was her motive? It still wasn't clear why George would have been a target.

The Millard house came into view as I crested a hill. It was old and in dire need of repair. At one time it was probably a very nice farmhouse, white with two stories and green-shuttered windows. Now, it was a ramshackle mess. The roof needed replacing, its shingles were buckled and falling off in places. The board and batten siding could use several new coats of paint. Outside on the front lawn, there was an old refrigerator and the shell of an old car rusting under the snow.

I parked my Nissan on the side of the road because the driveway was full of ice. I would have wondered if I had the right place, except there was an old wooden sign at the end of the driveway that said "Millard," in faded letters.

I grabbed the duffle bag and started down the icy driveway, determined now more than ever to make this a quick visit.

I stepped onto the porch and met with a menacing growl that made my scalp tingle.

I turned around to see an angry Rottweiler, licking his lips and showing his ugly, pointed teeth. I saw he had a chain around his neck, keeping him from lunging at me, and took some small relief from that.

"Nice doggy," I said nervously, knocking at the door.

There was no response, and I was growing more and more anxious. The Rottweiler started barking, sharp, angry staccato notes. Finally, the door opened, and Alvira stood in the doorway, looking dazed.

"Maddie?"

"Hi, Alvira! I'm just returning this bag you left at Aunt Cassie's house. Hope you haven't been missing it too much."

"Oh, thanks," she said, blinking. Her voice sounded strange. She stood for a moment, staring at me uncertainly. Then she seemed to snap out of it.

"Maddie, I'm glad you're here. Come in and have a cup of tea with me," she said, opening the door wide.

"Oh, no. I have to get back to Thalia's. She's expecting me."

"Please, just for a few minutes," Alvira pleaded. I relented, realizing how few visitors Alvira must get. This was obviously important to her.

I followed her into the kitchen. The place was dimly lit, and there were dirty dishes everywhere. I cringed, seeing cobwebs in the corners and dust and dirt in every crevice. My nurse's sensibilities required everything to be clean. This place was a hotbed of bacteria. The only upside to it was that Alvira must have a strong immune system to be able to fight off all the germs.

Alvira cleared off the table and invited me to sit while she made tea. I sat down and waited. And waited. She seemed to be taking a long time. I got up to stretch my legs a bit and look around the place.

There was a dirty living room with a decade-old couch and a few semi-valuable antiques. A fireplace added some interest to the corner, and there were photos on the mantlepiece, many of them were of Alvira, and her mother and some were school photos of Alvira growing up. I picked up one of the pictures which showed a smiling Alvira, much younger, with a smiling handsome young man.

"I've seen you before," I said under my breath. But where? Then it came to me. This young man was one of the Hunt Club members. Was this Matt, the young man Alex said she often flirted with? I listened for Alvira and heard her still moving around in the kitchen. Then I carefully slipped the photo out of the frame to look at the back. "My Steve," it said in a small, tight script, very different from Tuppence Millard's writing on the back of the Hunt Club photo. I sucked in my breath. Could Alvira's Steve be Steve Braeman from the Hunt Club? It seemed that Alex had got it wrong. It wasn't Matt that Alvira had been going out with. It was Steve Braeman, the young man who had been killed in the hunting accident.

The proverbial light-bulb began to go off in my head as I started piecing things together. I put the photo back in its frame and set it back on the fireplace, careful to return it to its original position.

If Steve had been Alvira's boyfriend, then Alvira had a convincing motive to kill John, who was in the Hunt Club and was thought to have fired the fatal shot. She also had reason to kill George, who was also in the Hunt Club and was instrumental in starting up the Hunt Club again.

I walked back to the table, my heart thumping wildly. I took a couple slow, deep breaths.

I thought about the portrait of John by Tuppence Millard. I only had Alvira's word for it that Tuppence was obsessed with John. Maybe Tuppence had painted the portrait as a tribute, just as she had said, and it was Alvira who had slashed the portrait in anger!

"I'm almost done, Maddie," sang Alvira from the kitchen. "I'm just getting us a snack to eat, too."

"Not a problem, take your time!" I called back, trying to keep the nerves out of my voice.

Alvira had slept over at Green Briar the night before the second murder, so she had ample opportunity to grab John's gun, slip out early in the morning and kill George in the forest while no one was expecting it. She had been around the Hunt Club and had watched her mother hunt, so it was likely she would know how to use a gun. She could have even faked her illness the night before so she would have an excuse to be there when the hunt started.

Yes, it all fit very well, I thought. I had no solid proof, but the pieces were all fitting into place. Now I had only one problem: I needed to get away without Alvira knowing I suspected anything.

CHAPTER THIRTY

Alvira brought out the tea, some pound cake and some assorted crackers with salmon dip. It looked very nice; I had to admit, but I was not at all hungry by this time. I was increasingly certain that this woman was the one who had poisoned my Uncle John's tea.

"Have a drink, Maddie. Go on," Alvira urged. "I made you lemon ginger—just like your Uncle John used to drink."

"Oh, no thank you, Alvira. I'm allergic to ginger," I lied.

"Oh, but you'll like this one, I promise," Alvira purred. "Just try it. Please? Or, why don't you have some crackers and salmon."

My stomach lurched.

"I'm not very hungry, Alvira. This was a bad idea. I'm sorry to have put you to all this trouble."

Alvira looked at me with narrowed cat's eyes, suddenly sly.

"Is there something wrong, Maddie?"

"Not at all," I said evenly. "I think it's these murders, Alvira. I haven't eaten or slept very well at all. Have you?"

"No, I guess not," said Alvira shrugging.

"Would you like to see the rest of the house?" She jumped up, looking excited suddenly like a child at Christmas.

"No, Alvira," I said firmly. "I really must go. My Mom and

Thalia are expecting me."

Alvira looked disappointed, then she shrugged.

"Okay. Whatever. Maybe you'll come back and visit another time?"

"Sure, Alvira," I said, breathing a sigh of relief. I went to the door to get my boots on.

"You know what? I'll just wrap up some cake and crackers so that you can have some later when you're hungry. Wait here— I'll be right back."

She grabbed the food off the table and went back into the kitchen to wrap it up.

I hesitated at the door. I could run out the door and make my escape now, but Alvira would know something was amiss. I had to wait until she came back with the treats.

While I was waiting, I saw a piece of paper on the floor. It must have fallen off the table when Alvira cleared it earlier. I picked it up and looked at it. When I realized what it was, my hands started shaking. It was another photo of the Hunt Club, very much like the one in Alvira's make-up bag, only this one had a scratch over John and George's faces. I felt sick. Suddenly, I heard a click by my head and froze.

"Turn around slowly," a raspy voice whispered in my ear.

I turned around obediently and saw Alvira behind me, framed in the light of the kitchen. Alvira stood there, holding a hunting rifle—probably belonging to her mother.

"I'll take that, thanks," said Alvira, one hand ripping the photo out of my hands.

"I'm not stupid, Maddie. I knew you were beginning to suspect me. Now, my mother is asleep upstairs. If you wake her, or if you scream, I will shoot," she said in a low voice. "Make no mistake about it."

Alvira's hair had fallen around her shoulders, and her eyes

were wild. She did not look like the Alvira I thought I knew. Her jaw was set, and her eyes were cold and cunning. Her very features had changed. What demon had possessed her, for her to look like this?

"Alvira, what are you doing?" I asked quietly. "This isn't you."

"How do you know what is and isn't me, Bitch," she growled. Her lip curled into a sneer. I stared at her in shock. She was obviously insane. I don't know how I never suspected that before.

"I never liked you, you know," Alvira spat. "I only pretended. You're a bloody little minx with Alex tied around your little finger. He and I went out a few times. When you came, that all went out the window. I never had a chance with you around. Though, of course, he's not a patch on my Steve."

"I didn't know you liked Alex... you should have told me," I said softly.

"Shut up, Maddie, you liar! I'm so glad you came today—you were meant to die next. You deserve it! You deserve to die, just like John and George."

"For Steve's death? Alvira, what happened to Steve was an accident. It was nobody's fault."

"I said, shut up!" shouted Alvira pressing the barrel of the gun to my ribs, where my heart was still pounding. I prayed that Tuppence would hear her, but I wondered what she would do if she did.

"I am going to keep my gun pointed at you, and you're going to walk with me to your car. Then you're going to take me back to Green Briar, to your little cottage in the woods. If you make a noise, I will shoot, so keep your damned mouth shut." Alvira jabbed the barrel of the rifle into the back of my ribs. I straightened up slowly and headed for the door.

"Get going!" urged Alvira giving me a push. I stumbled, then turned the knob. We shuffled out into the snow.

Alvira made me drive so that she could keep the gun firmly pointed at me. We drove in silence. I was afraid to say anything that would set her off. That was the longest drive of my life.

Finally, we reached Green Briar. I parked the car close to the house as Alvira directed me to, then we walked around the side of the ranch house to the forest in the back. Before we disappeared around the side, I glanced over at the barn. The light was on. I wondered if Alex was inside, and whether he had seen the car coming down the drive. It filled me with hope. Surely Alex would notice my car and wonder why I was back at Green Briar. I prayed he would notice in time.

The walk through the forest seemed to take forever. Everything seemed hyper-bright to my senses. I looked around at the trees, breathing in the crisp air. My breathing sounded amplified in my ears. Alvira didn't make a sound, but every so often the barrel of the gun jabbed at me painfully, letting me know she was still there.

Finally, we reached the door of the cottage. It was locked. Alvira took out a key and opened the door.

"I bet you didn't know this was used as a hunting cabin at one time," Alvira gloated. "All the Hunt Club members had a key. I got this one from my mother."

Alvira pushed me inside and made me sit on one of the wooden chairs by the table in the window. She ripped off the pretty curtain that Cassie had made and used the cord to tie me to the chair, tight enough to keep me there for a while, but not tight enough to leave any marks on my skin.

"You know," said Alvira finishing the job by stuffing the rags in my mouth, "I would often stay out here before you came. Just watching, biding my time. Watching that horrid little man go about his business, the murderer of my Steve. I had some fun, though. Poisoning his cattle with Oleander leaves, practicing for the big day." Alvira laughed smugly. It turned my stomach sick.

I looked her in the eye. "It was you who set fire to this cottage, wasn't it?"

Alvira sniffed. "That was an accident. I was lighting a candle in honor of Steve. He likes it when I do that. He knows I haven't forgotten him," she said softly. "I must have left it burning that one time. Careless of me. I lost my best picture of him with his snakehead bandana." Her eyes turned sly again. "Wish I had burned down the whole cabin. Maybe you would have just gone back home."

Then Alvira turned her back on me and went into the kitchen. I could hear her filling the kettle with water.

"You see, Maddie, you're going to have a nice cup of tea. Only this tea will have oleander in it, just like John's. I keep some in my pocket for occasions such as this one." Alvira practically bounced with glee. "I do love oleander flowers. I have a lot of it growing in the back of my house. It was the easiest thing to poison John. He was so stupid! I gave him the oleander petals mixed with rose petals. He loved trying herbs for his health you know. When I told him the rose petals would help his arthritis, he agreed to try them in his tea!"

She laughed maniacally. "How lovely it was to see John retching, to see him go red and blistery, grasping his stomach in pain. It felt so good to avenge Steve's death! He was the only one who ever really loved me, you know." She looked at me with a cruel smile.

"Oh, this will be so easy! I understand you get pretty depressed sometimes," she sneered. "You will be very depressed tonight, my dear Maddie, and you will take your own life. But first, you will write a nice suicide note."

She took a scrap of paper from the wastepaper basket, one of the balled-up poems that I had rejected and smoothed it out. Then she held the barrel of the gun to my chest as I obediently wrote my suicide note:

"Shakespeare wrote that all the world is a stage. If this is so, I will exit now, bidding you farewell. All you cruel actors, with your Viral hatred, this is goodbye." I cringed. It was terrible writing, but if I died here in this way, I was going to leave a clue leading to my murderer. I hoped at least Alex would figure out about one actor, who had Viral in her name.

Alvira read it and snorted with laughter. "You fancy yourself a poet, don't you? Pathetic." She slapped the note down on the table. "Time for tea, Maddie."

I had to think fast. I wasn't about to become Alvira's third victim. I tried to wiggle my hands and feet out of the ropes. It turned out to be easier than I thought. Alvira was delusional. For some reason, she thought I would sit there passively and wait for death. She was sorely mistaken. I grabbed an iron pot from the wood stove and brought it down on her the moment she left the kitchen before she could have time to point the gun at me. The oleander tea went crashing to the floor. Alvira went down with it. The only thing I hadn't counted on was that the gun also hit the floor and went off with a deafening sound, its bullet grazing my shoulder. I screamed bloody murder, and then the door flew open.

Through the waves of pain, I saw Alex holding his rifle, followed by Tuppence Millard and a flurry of police and first-responders.

My shoulder was bandaged, and I was given an injection for pain. The police questioned me about Alvira, and I told them what I knew. Then they took her away, and I lost consciousness.

CHAPTER THIRTY-ONE

I found out I made a horrible patient. It was strange, seeing the hospital from a patient's point of view. If I decided to go back to nursing, I would be a lot more sympathetic to patient complaints. Recovering from a shoulder wound was a long and difficult process.

The doctors at St. Joseph's Hospital in Reidsville gave excellent care. One doctor, in particular, visited me often. I tried hard to discourage him, but he was very persistent.

"Clayton, you don't have to do this," I said as he came bearing flowers, once again, to cheer me up. "Besides, what a patient needs to cheer her up, is chocolate," I hinted.

"Sweets for my sweet," said Clayton, presenting me with a box of After Eights.

"You read my mind!" I smiled. Then I took a deep breath. I needed to be serious.

"Clayton, you really are wonderful. But I'm not sure I want or deserve all this attention. Besides, I think Detective Inspector Trent has taken quite a liking to you," I threw him a shrewd look. He shook his head.

"No, it's not what you think," he said smiling. "Rebecca's a cousin of mine. We've always been good friends." He grinned.

"You were jealous, weren't you? Admit it."

"No!" I cried, a little too vehemently. "Well, okay, maybe. But not as much as I thought I would be," I said smiling, but not on the inside. I needed to tell him something and it wouldn't be easy for me to say, or for him to hear.

Clayton sat at my bedside, smoothing back my hair. I admit, it felt wonderful to be with him. There was a chemistry between us, a fire... I could give into that flame, but I was afraid it would eventually fizzle out, and I would end up getting burned. I had made up my mind, and it was time to let him know what I had decided.

"Clayton, I've been doing a lot of thinking ..." I began.

"Oh no. Maddie, don't say it..."

"I have to. I've been hinting around about it, but I've just got to say it: I think we should stop seeing each other." I clenched my fists so hard, my nails dug into the palms of my hands. There. It was done.

He stared at me for a moment, a mixture of emotions on his face; pain, sadness, disbelief.

"I won't lie to you. That hurts." He grimaced. "You've decided for Alex, then?"

I was silent for a minute. Then I nodded.

"Yes. We know each other really well. We have a history together. You and I—it's just an attraction. That's not enough for a lifetime."

Clayton shook his head and sighed. "You're wrong." He leaned over the bed to look into my eyes. "You know what I think, Maddie? I think you're just afraid. I think we have something special, and it's not just physical. We were meant to be together. I really believe that." His blue eyes blazed. I had to look away.

For a brief moment, I wavered; for one split second, uneasiness robbed my heart of the peace that I had felt. What if he was right? He seemed so sure… But I had made my decision. Life was full of hard decisions. I was sure that I had made the right one: I had to be strong.

Clayton's hand found mine and he gave it a squeeze. "I'm going away, Maddie, but I'm not giving up on you. Time will prove I'm right."

"Good bye Clayton," I whispered, closing my eyes. I kept them closed, until I heard his footsteps ebb away.

CHAPTER THIRTY-TWO

I slept after that, for hours and hours; easy to do with the amount of morphine I was taking. I opened my eyes to see Alex watching me from the doorway, leaning against the frame. The look of concerned devotion on his face made my heart ache for him.

"Hi," I said groggily, trying to sit up, then yelping in pain.

"You're hurting—should I call someone?" Alex rushed over to my side.

"No, it's okay," I said, smiling at him. "It's only when I first get up. Besides, they have me on enough morphine to down an elephant."

"When do you think they'll let you out of here?" he asked, taking the chair beside me.

"Not for at least another month, Doc says." I sighed.

"Do you know, Tuppence sent me a card?"

"Really?" Alex's eyebrows shot up.

"Yep. She says she's sorry for everything Alvira has done. She suspected her daughter was insane for a long time but hadn't the heart to do anything about it. She didn't want to believe it."

"Well, I can't forgive her for allowing two murders," said Alex, his eyes clouding over. "John would still be alive if she had spoken up sooner. And you could have died."

"At least Tuppence tried to save my life. She heard Alvira talking to me and saw her point the gun at me at the Millard place, when Alvira thought she was upstairs asleep. After we left for Green Briar, she got the police."

"Yeah, I saw your car pull up at the ranch, and knew something was up. I was already on my way to find you when Tuppence came with the police. But I needn't have worried—it looked like you had things pretty well in hand."

"In my shoulder, you mean," I said teasingly. Alex smiled.

"What do you think will happen to Alvira?" I asked, suddenly serious.

"I think she won't have to stand trial. I think it's likely she'll be judged incompetent and be institutionalized."

I was silent for a moment. Then I said, "I do feel sorry for her, you know. I think she was grieving, and then the grief turned to hate. Hatred can twist the mind to evil. That's when she lost touch with reality—"

My voice trailed off. I knew what it was to look over the edge of reality, but thankfully I had never stepped over that edge. No matter how manic I was, or how depressed I got, I could still choose right from wrong, light from darkness. I had to believe that in spite of everything, I would always stay in the light.

Alex took my hand and gently stroked my fingers. He looked as though he wanted to say something but couldn't find the words. I didn't need words. I just needed him close to me.

Then Alex's gaze fell on the fresh flowers in the window and his eyes narrowed. "Dr. Manning has been here again, I see," he said bitterly, drawing his hand away.

"Alex Bateman, are you jealous?" I asked, teasing.

He looked at me, dead serious. "I am. I can't help it, Maddie. I'm trying to be just a friend, but it's not working very well. It's tearing me up inside."

I studied him sitting beside me, his elbow leaning on the bedrail and his head leaning dejectedly on his hand. The shock of brown hair fell forward over his face but didn't obscure his dark blue eyes, narrowed in pain. My heart swelled.

"I don't think I can handle it anymore, either, Alex," I said, my voice breaking. "You've always been a good friend, but lately, I've had deeper feelings for you."

He lifted his head slowly.

"Are you saying what I think you're saying?" he said, raising his eyes to look at mine. A new light danced in their depths.

I smiled and nodded. Alex's face broke into the sweetest smile, like the sun breaking through the clouds. It took my breath away. He leaned over me, his nose brushing my cheek.

"Kiss me," he said. "Like you mean it." So I did.

ABOUT THE AUTHOR

Raven McKray lives in Ontario, Canada. She received her master's degree in English Literature from Carleton University and has a degree in Education from the University of Ottawa. Her first novel, "Under A Fairy Moon," written under the pseudonym "T. M. Wallace" won the Gelett Burgess Children's Book Award (Fantasy) and the Canadian Christian Writer's Award (Young Adult Fiction) in 2012. "A Twist of Oleander" is her first mystery novel for adults.

A NOTE FROM THE AUTHOR

I hope you enjoyed reading A Twist of Oleander. If you liked this book, please consider writing a review for it on Amazon or Goodreads. I appreciate your comments and suggestions.

The second book in the series is "Death Comes Whispering," in which Maddie must solve the murder of Spooky Joe McConnell, found drowned in the Whispering Woods of Kenowa.

You can visit my website, www.ravenmckray.com for updates and sample chapters.

Many Blessings,

Raven McKray